46

D0724535

From the doorway of the barn, Cole had seen Brianna's horse slam into a delicately built woman and throw her into the wall.

During the seconds it took to reach her, he'd prayed for her safety, his fear mounting when she slumped against the oak paneling, her face shadowed beneath the bill of her cap.

Just as he was about to put a hand on her shoulder, she pulled off the cap, revealing her trademark McAllister hair—an unusual burnished strawberry blond—and an all too familiar dusting of freckles across her nose.

Leigh.

A barrage of old emotions hit him like a sucker punch to the gut. Anger. Hurt. And a feeling of betrayal so deep that it still made his heart ache whenever he thought about his father's unjust imprisonment...and the McAllisters whose testimony had put him there.

Books by Roxanne Rustand

Love Inspired Suspense

*Hard Evidence #81
*Vendetta #87

*Snow Canyon Ranch

ROXANNE RUSTAND,

an award-winning author of sixteen books, feels delighted and honored at the opportunity to write for Steeple Hill Love Inspired Suspense.

Her first manuscript won a Romance Writers of America Golden Heart Award for Best Long Contemporary. Her second was a Golden Heart Award finalist and was published in 1999. She has presented workshops at writers' conferences from coast to coast and is a member of the American Christian Fiction Writers Association, the Faith, Hope and Love Chapter of RWA, Authors Guild, and Novelists Inc.

She has a master's degree in nutrition and works as a registered dietitian for a residential psychiatric facility. She and her husband live on an acreage in the Midwest and have three children, two semiretired horses, a couple of goofy border collies and a number of very demanding cats. Roxanne loves to hear from readers and can be reached through www.shoutlife.com/roxannerustand or by snail mail at Box 2550, Cedar Rapids, Iowa 52406.

Though the mountains leave their place and the hills
be shaken, My love will never leave you.
—*Isaiah* 54:10

Published by

With many thanks to wonderful editors
Krista Stroever and Johanna Raisanen
for giving me this opportunity to write for
Love Inspired Suspense!

ONE

Four Winds Ranch lay in the valley below, rimmed to the west by the Wyoming Rockies. Lush meadows spread like emerald blankets among stands of pine and aspen. Even from this mountain road, Cole Daniels could see the sparkling water of a stream that meandered from a high canyon and traversed the property. His property, now.

Postcard perfect, the ranch represented everything he'd ever worked for, everything he'd lost—and a nightmare that had lasted for sixteen long years.

But now he was back, and he was going to make things right.

Grim memories assaulted him as he shifted his pickup into gear and dróve down to the home place, where a construction crew was framing up a new fifty-by-eighty-foot horse barn and refurbishing the old one.

Irwin Benson, the crew boss, nodded to Cole

and strolled over to his truck, offering his hand for an overly hearty shake. "It's coming along."

The crew of eight had stopped to watch them, but when Cole returned their stares, they all turned back to work. "Will it be done by Labor Day?"

"Maybe." Irwin pushed up the brim of his ball cap and mopped at the sweat on his brow. "If we get the materials in time."

Cole narrowed his gaze on Irwin's face. "I thought everything was ordered a month ago."

"I did, just as promised." Irwin shifted his weight and looked away. "The siding hasn't come, and the hardware for the sliding stall doors is still on back order."

"Is there a reason?"

"Just some sort of delay. That's all they told me."

"When is it supposed to arrive?"

Irwin shrugged. "I didn't get a straight answer. I did check with some other suppliers in the area, but then we'd be starting all over. And if they've got back orders, too…"

"I'll stop in Wolf Creek and talk to the lumber-yard manager." Cole thought back to his senior year of high school, sorting through the names and faces that he could still remember. But after so many years of trying to forget this town and everyone in it, many of its inhabitants were just a dim memory. "Is it still owned by the Olsons?"

"Yep, so good luck." A faint smirk twisted Irwin's

mouth, but quickly faded. "They were good friends of Wes Truly, you know."

"Really."

"Not to say they'd hold a grudge or anything, but some people just don't forget."

Cole stilled, a deadly calm spreading through him. "What about you?"

The older man's eyes flared wider, as if he'd suddenly realized his mistake—and now faced danger he hadn't expected. He held out his hands, fingers splayed. "All of that's old business. Nothing to do with me back then, and not now, either."

Cole bared his teeth in a smile. "But you were around in those days. Right?"

"Er…guess I was. But I had no stake in anything that happened." Irwin nodded vigorously. "I…liked Rand. A lot." He cast a nervous glance over his shoulder. "I better get to work, so we can get the windows framed up before we leave today."

Cole watched the man head back to the barn. There'd be other days, other chances to see how much Irwin really knew. And before the barn was finished, Cole planned to have conversations with every last man on the crew. Unlike the people in town, they were temporarily in his employ…which meant he had a better chance at getting them to talk.

Sixteen years ago a jury had convicted his father of murder, and two years later, he'd died in prison.

At least two of the witnesses had lied.

But someone in this town had to know the truth.

If it took the rest of his life, Cole was going to find out what had really happened that night, because despite local opinion, Rand Daniels had died an innocent man.

Leigh McAllister had dreamed of this day throughout all four years of vet school.

Planned every last detail. Felt her anticipation rising with every long-distance call from her uncle Gray, who'd offered her space for a clinic at Four Winds, his Wyoming ranch.

The news of his unexpected death last winter had left her grieving for months.

She'd finally rallied over the summer. Found another place to begin her practice. But now, with a hot August wind kicking up dust devils across the desolate parking lot and everything she owned packed in the back of her ancient pickup, Leigh wasn't sure if the precious contract in her hand was an opportunity or a life sentence of debt.

The weathered building ahead of her had seen better days. Much of the veterinary equipment inside was outdated. And the blue-sky part of the practice—the warmth and skill of the county's beloved Doc Henry Adams—would be moving with him to Arizona at the end of the week.

Yet the Wolf Creek Vet Clinic had always been

the busiest practice in two counties, and the client base alone had to be pure gold.

Unless Neil's warnings were true.

Remembering the phone call from Henry's nephew a few weeks ago, she closed her eyes. *Dear Lord, please let this practice be Your answer to my prayers, and not just my own blind desire.*

She turned at the sound of wheels crunching across the gravel and squinted against the glaring Wyoming sun, its rays all the more blinding at this altitude.

A gleaming Ford pickup pulled to a stop a few yards away from her, sending a cloud of thick dust boiling into the air. Through the haze, she could make out Salt Grass Veterinary Services—Neil Adams, DVM emblazoned in script on the side of the multi-compartment vet box installed in the bed of the truck.

Henry climbed out of the passenger side, his white hair thick as ever, his jaunty stride belying his seventy-five years.

Another twinge of doubt worked its way through her midsection and began to tie her stomach into a knot. Had she ever really imagined that she could replace him?

He batted at the dust with one big paw. "Sorry about that, Leigh. My nephew might be a dandy vet, but he's still got hot-rodding in his soul."

"I remember," she retorted with a dry laugh, recalling the freckle-faced boy who'd had half the charm and common sense of his uncle, and far too much money to burn. "High school, senior year. Neil rolled his new Corvette going over High Creek Pass."

"Two weeks off the showroom floor." Henry's voice held a note of amused affection. "Didn't even have a bruise, but his daddy sure hit the ceiling." The twinkle in his eyes faded. "Real sorry about your uncle, by the way. It's hard to believe he's gone."

"Thanks. I miss him so much."

Neil stepped out of the truck and pulled a ball cap over his sandy, thinning hair. "Everything settled?"

"Just need a quick walk-through." Henry tossed a ring of keys to Leigh. "I want to make sure everything is in good shape."

Neil glanced at his watch. "Fifteen minutes, and Aunt Martha wants you home."

Henry waved dismissively. "She's probably already ordering those movers around like a drill sergeant. I'll just be in the way."

He led them into the clinic, through the waiting room with its brown tiled floor and bare windows facing the mountains to the west. Past the tall counter separating the receptionist's area, with its banks of file cabinets and an old-fashioned typewriter.

Rustic pine paneling and framed Remington prints gave way to off-white walls and bright fluorescent lighting in the hall leading to the heart of the building—the two exam rooms, a lab and phar-macy, storeroom, treatment area, surgery and an office. Beyond another door was a tiny apartment that would be her home for the foreseeable future.

"I'm leaving decent, usable equipment that oughta hold you for awhile." Henry braced a hand on the doorway to the lab and sighed heavily. From his long face, this last visit was more like a wake than a joyous departure into the freedom of retirement. "Once you have my old vet box mounted in the bed of your truck, you should be good to go."

"I'm just thankful for everything that was in-cluded in our deal." She stepped past him and walked along the long white counter filled with lab equipment. Above, glass-front cupboards revealed bags of sterilized surgical instruments resting in stainless-steel trays, ready for action. Beyond the refrigerator, shelves of pharmaceuticals filled the rest of the back wall.

Neil met and held Leigh's gaze, but waited until his uncle walked down the hall and disappeared into one of the exam rooms. "This isn't going to be an easy transition for you."

"Believe me, I never thought it would be."

"He was an institution in these parts, and my practice in Salt Grass is just forty miles away." Neil cleared his throat. "Two strikes against someone new. And honestly, he should have retired years ago."

Unease slithered through her midsection. "Why?"

"Well…" Neil lowered his voice. "Errors in judgment. A few mistakes. Might've just been his vision…but either way, he was losing business. Fast."

That sense of unease now wrapped around her heart and tightened like a vise. "But I saw the figures—the gross last year was almost $190k."

"Was it?" Neil gave her a thin smile. "*Really?* But the bigger question is how much higher was it the year before, and the year before that?" He glanced at a water-stained area in the ceiling tile. "And how much will it take to repair this old place? You, my dear, have just boarded a sinking ship."

She'd needed to come back to Wolf Creek because of family problems, but this clinic hadn't been a snap decision. She'd prayed long and hard about it over the past six months. She'd spent hours researching banks and meeting with loan officers before she'd signed the contract.

And now, her uneasiness turned to fear.

She had no choice. She *had* to make money—and she had to start making it fast.

To help her get started, Henry had offered to sell his practice on a one-year, lease-to-own deal, with a balloon payment in twelve months.

Already she was facing over eight hundred dollars a month on the practice, the used truck she'd needed to buy last year, and a short-term loan on some extra equipment and supplies. Once her student loan deferment ended in three months, the figure would jump to over eleven hundred.

And if she didn't keep up with her payments, no bank on earth would consider financing the practice come next fall. Which meant she could lose…everything.

Neil must have read her mind, because he smiled in sympathy. "Not good news, I know. Just don't forget—my offer still stands."

She nodded faintly.

A merger of the two veterinary practices was probably the most logical plan, but it was one she would never consider. She knew what would happen. One more person would end up calling the shots, and it wouldn't be her. Her lifelong goal of independence would slip from her grasp.

And then she'd never be able to prove her worth to the one person she'd never been able to please.

By Tuesday morning, Leigh had cleaned the clinic from one end to the other. Inventoried and organized the existing supplies. Met with a veterinary supply company sales rep to order additional pharmaceuticals and surgical equipment.

She'd lingered over his catalogs long after the sales rep had left, lost in wishful thinking about a new anesthesia machine and the latest models of portable X-rays. Maybe next year…

She and her two sisters had shared in their late

uncle Gray's modest inheritance. With her own portion, she'd made a substantial payment on her college loan, but with another fifty grand left on that plus her debt on the practice, exciting new equipment would definitely have to wait.

At the ring of the telephone she jumped to her feet, the catalogs flying. Her first client?

It was—but when he gave her directions, she nearly dropped the phone.

"F-Four Winds?" She gripped the receiver tighter, struggling for control as memories threatened to swamp her. "Are you the new owner?"

"Max, his ranch hand. Look, Doc Henry has been out several times since my boss bought the place. But if there's a problem…"

"No, not at all. I—I just need to pull the file." She spun toward the file cabinets, found the F-G-H drawer and thumbed over the name tabs until she found the manila folder for the ranch. Her heart caught when she realized that the documents inside still bore her late uncle Gray's name. "For some reason, the new owner isn't listed."

"Daniels. But he ain't here right now. He's on his way home from California."

"*Daniels?*" Stunned, she held her breath, hoping she'd heard wrong. "*Cole* Daniels?"

"You got it."

She ran a hand through her hair and noticed her fingers were shaking. Cole was *back?*

The man snickered. "Lotta folks in these parts are gonna be mighty surprised when they see a Daniels back in town, eh? Another McAllister, for that matter. So, when can you get out here?"

She could hardly turn down her first call. Not when the nearest vet was Neil, who was another forty miles away. And definitely not after he'd gently warned her that she might ultimately fail. "I—I'll be there in forty-five minutes."

Bowing her head, she hung up the phone and braced her palms on the desk, remembering Cole. A long-ago murder. The nightmares that still had the power to leave her shaking.

And she prayed she wouldn't encounter the man who'd once broken her heart.

Twenty miles out of town on narrow, curving roads, Four Winds shared a mile of backcountry fence line with her mother's Snow Canyon Ranch. The original family property had been a vast, sprawling ranch during the days of the Wyoming frontier, but had been divided between Gray and her mother after the death of their father.

Widowed twice after stormy, ill-fated marriages, Claire had soldiered on alone, taking back the McAllister name for herself and her three young daughters. She'd ruled her half of the ranch with an iron hand, driving it to success with little time or thought for the usual niceties of motherhood.

To Claire's obvious disgust, her older brother Gray had shared none of her blind ambition. He'd taken a steadier course, by marrying a sweet young woman from a prominent ranching family and welcoming their assistance and advice, and he'd ended up far more successful.

Happier, too. A man with a good marriage and strong faith, the only regret he'd ever voiced was that he'd never been blessed with children.

Ironic, Leigh thought as she turned up the long lane leading to the main buildings at Four Winds. After decades of an edgy undercurrent of competition between Claire and Gray, where were they now?

Uncle Gray and Aunt Betty were gone. Old and bitter, Claire was sliding into dementia, without any close friends and resentful of her daughters' efforts to help her. She'd always figured her daughters would inherit Four Winds someday, and that the land would stay in the family. Instead, Gray had abruptly sold it to a company in California just before he'd died, then most of the money from the sale had mysteriously disappeared.

Claire was still furious over her brother's betrayal and refused to discuss it.

Topping the last rise before descending to the home place of Four Winds, Leigh slammed on the brakes and stared.

The ranch was nestled in the shadow of the Rockies, breathtakingly beautiful as ever, with its log-and-stone two-story house and pretty pastures rimmed with aspen and pine.

But the familiar buildings were different, and now there were new corrals and an arena, all enclosed with white, three-plank fencing—a jarring change from everything she remembered. Tension knotted her stomach as she wondered what Cole would say if he saw her here. Did he even know that she was the vet who had been summoned? *Please Lord, let Cole be away from this ranch today....*

But her tension was soon tempered with melancholy as she drove on down to the main barn. While her sister Tessa had been their mother's shadow and Janna had always been immersed in her books, the happiest moments of Leigh's own childhood had centered on Uncle Gray and Aunt Betty's ranch. It had been the one place where a youngest, largely ignored daughter could feel loved and special. And now...everything in that beloved past had changed.

A weathered cowboy in a battered hat—definitely not Cole—appeared at the door and motioned her inside.

Breathing a sigh of relief, she pulled on her ball cap, grabbed her portable X-ray unit from the back of her truck and strolled into the barn. A thin, dejected-looking horse stood cross-tied in the aisle, his front legs extended slightly beyond the vertical.

From the looks of his long, badly cracked hooves,

he hadn't seen a farrier in six months, and from the appearance of his coat, he hadn't seen decent feed in that amount of time, either. If his stance was any clue, she suspected there'd be some bad news on the X-rays she took today. "You're Max?"

"Yep. And this is…uh…Filbert," the cowboy offered with a derisive snort. "Navicular, we think."

"Looks suspicious to me, too. They often stand that way to relieve the pain in their heels. Is…um… your boss going to be back soon?"

"Yep. But you can deal with me." He leaned against a stall door, watching her with doubtful, narrowed eyes. "You look mighty young to be a vet."

She'd expected that. Expected hesitance over her being a woman, as well, in this very rural area, even though more women than men graduated from vet school every year and that ratio was steadily rising.

"I've got the degree to prove it," she said with a smile before hunkering next to the horse's front legs to begin her examination. "Plus a year of postgraduate internship in equine medicine."

"So we'll have to call someone else for the cattle?"

"Nope. I planned on a mixed large- and small-animal practice." She finished palpating the gelding's joints, then straightened, picked up his near foreleg and began cleaning away the loose debris from his sole. "I'll work on anything except exotics."

Beneath the debris she found a significant case of thrush—evidence of unclean stalls and poor care.

The new fences and buildings here were beautiful. Cole's father had been a horse trainer, and as a young man, Cole had been successful on the rodeo circuit. He ought to know how to care for his animals. That he was providing such poor care for this one sparked her anger.

She nodded toward the duffel she'd brought in with the X-ray unit. "Hand me the hoof tester, would you?"

Max fished out the tool, which was shaped like pliers with twelve-inch handles, and handed it to her.

"Thanks. I hope—" From the corner of her eye, Leigh saw something small, white and scraggly burst into the barn amid a furious volley of barks.

And then came the sound of running feet and the anxious calls of a child in hot pursuit. "Sammy! Oh, Sammy—please come back!"

The dog hesitated for a split second, barked all the louder and raced between the gelding's front feet. Then both the dog and a young girl with a chestnut ponytail flew down the aisle and disappeared.

Filbert snorted, jerked back and reared. The cross ties snapped to his halter held him back, and he fought wildly against the ropes, his back hooves scrambling and sliding on the concrete as if the surface were made of ice.

"Easy, boy. Easy," Leigh crooned, reaching for his halter and soothing him with a steadying hand on his neck.

He lunged forward, then tried to rear again—this time, crashing sideways into her before she could step clear.

The barn seemed to spin in a dizzying rush.

She felt weightless. Disoriented. Then she landed with a resounding *smack* on the floor, against the door of a stall.

It took a moment for her head to stop spinning.

From somewhere far away, she heard the ranch hand's voice tinged with a hint of derision.

"…yeah, it's the new vet. Came out instead of Doc Adams. She's quite a pro, all right."

A large, dark shadow moved in front of her, blocked out the bright fluorescent lighting along the aisle. A hand reached out and rested on her shoulder, sending an oddly familiar sensation of warmth through her.

"Are you okay, ma'am?"

She blinked. And saw her own shock and wariness mirrored in Cole Daniels's eyes.

TWO

From the doorway of the barn, Cole had seen Brianna's horse slam into a delicately built woman and throw her into the wall. During the seconds it took to reach her, he prayed fast and hard for her safety, his fear mounting when she slumped against the oak paneling, her face shadowed beneath the bill of her cap.

By the time he touched her shoulder, she'd pulled off the cap, revealing her trademark McAllister looks—the unusual, burnished strawberry-blond hair and green eyes that she and her sisters shared, and an all too familiar dusting of freckles across her nose.

Leigh.

A barrage of old emotions hit him like a sucker punch to the gut. Anger. Hurt. An unwanted spark of attraction.

And a feeling of betrayal so deep that it still made his heart ache whenever he thought about his father's unjust imprisonment…and the two McAllisters whose testimony had put him there.

His faith shaken, Cole had prayed for justice… but it hadn't been served. He'd prayed for a sense of peace and understanding, but while his pain had muted over time, he still hadn't ever been able to fully let it go, and forgive the people who'd destroyed his family was still beyond him.

"This is quite a surprise, finding you here," he said, once he managed to control the simmering anger in his voice.

Leigh refused his hand and rose to her feet. "Max called the clinic," she said. "I'm here for a lameness exam."

Cole was speechless for a moment, as her words registered and the past sixteen years stretched out between them. Of course, he wasn't the same person he'd been, either. "You're a *vet?*"

"Yes, I am. I bought Doc Adams's practice."

It hardly seemed possible. She'd been the fun-loving, giddy one of the three McAllister girls—a little shy, yet eager to make friends—and at sixteen he'd been completely entranced by her silvery laugh and sweet nature, sure that he was falling in love. That she'd been able to buckle down into a difficult college program surprised him.

Max stood at the gelding's shoulder. The look he gave Cole suggested that he didn't trust her abilities, but the man clearly hadn't hung around the high-school rodeos so many years ago, when Cole had ridden bulls and Leigh had run barrels on some half-wild mare her mother had bought off a track. Leigh had been a superb horsewoman back then, and maybe she would be a good vet. But the thought of her coming to Four Winds on veterinary calls rankled.

Then again, maybe it wouldn't hurt to have some professional contact with the woman who symbolized everything that had gone wrong with his life so long ago. Eventually, she might be a source of information.

"I'll finish up, if that's okay." Her eyes narrowed with obvious suspicion. "But I'm curious—I heard an investment company bought this ranch. There was never any mention of your name."

"I own the company." Cole shrugged. "My lawyer handled the details."

She stiffened. "Uncle Gray loved this place. He told us it would always stay in the family."

Actually, when Cole's local Realtor had started scouting for property in the area last fall, Gray had been one of several ranchers selling out, and he'd been desperate for a sale. But he'd also demanded a promise that his reasons be kept private.

Cole had felt a certain sense of vindication at being able to buy out his old nemesis. But no matter what his low opinions were about the McAllisters, he was still honor-bound to keep his word.

"It's no secret that there are some hard feelings

between your family and mine." Leigh met his eyes with searing intensity in her own, a hint of bitterness in her voice. "So, are you planning on turning this beautiful place into condos or a resort?"

From her tone, she might as well have asked if he intended to develop a landfill. "If I did, it would be a business decision, not any sort of revenge." He nodded toward the framework of the new barn. "I'll be opening a horse-breeding and training facility as soon as everything is ready."

"You sure need to evaluate your feeding and worming program, then," she retorted, running a hand over Filbert's ribs. "This poor guy hasn't been well cared for at all."

"The boss knows what he's doing," Max snapped. Alarmed at his tone, the horse tossed his head and danced in place. "This horse was—"

Cole glanced at Max and lifted a hand, effectively silencing him. Maybe Leigh still thought he was dirt, but he didn't care. He didn't plan to explain himself to her or anyone else. "We'll handle it."

"Really?" She gave Cole a sharp glance, and her voice turned cold. "When was he last wormed? Or isn't that something you believe in?"

"Trust me, you don't need to ask." He thrust out his hand, just to aggravate her. "Look, I need to get going. Max can help you finish up."

She hesitated, then accepted a brief handshake, though she stepped back as if she'd touched fire.

His gesture backfired—because that brief touch sent a tingle of awareness dancing up his arm that reminded him of the single kiss they'd shared behind the chutes at a high-school rodeo. A kiss that had made him fall even deeper in love; made him feel so powerful that he could conquer the world—

Until she'd lied on the witness stand, and everything in his life had fallen into cinders at his feet.

He turned for the door. "I'm still commuting between here and California quite often. If we ever call you again, you'll work with Max. Brianna? Time to go."

He heard his daughter's booted feet follow him out the barn door, but he didn't look back. Once outside, he took a deep breath of pine-scented air before continuing toward the house.

Leigh had been the prettiest girl in school, and she'd been as far beyond his reach as the stars, given that she was a McAllister. Her mother and uncle had made that crystal clear. Now, her frosty businesslike manner took him aback.

But you've changed, too, he reminded himself. And few of those changes were for the better. The bad blood between his father and Gray McAllister had taken its toll in far too many ways. Maybe Gray had exacted his perfect retribution—but at what cost?

Looking out over a crowded courtroom, he'd spewed one lie after another, effectively sealing the fate of his old rival on the cutting-horse circuit. Then he'd smugly descended the witness stand and continued on with his life.

And then Leigh had been on that stand, too—to confirm every word the old snake had said.

Maybe it was too late for justice.

No. Cole was finally back, and he wasn't the same teenage boy overwhelmed by circumstances beyond his control. He was going to search until he found the truth.

And he was going to prove every one of those people wrong.

"I can hardly believe the work you've done." Awed, Leigh turned slowly, taking in the glittering antler chandeliers that cast a rich golden glow on the pine logs soaring high overhead in the lobby of her sister Janna's Snow Canyon Lodge. "After so many years empty, this place must have been in terrible shape."

Draped in colorful Navajo throws, a collection of soft, leather-upholstered sofas and chairs were arranged in conversational groupings near the massive stone fireplace. A wall of windows met the open beams above and faced a breathtaking view of the Rockies.

"Some of the cabins still need a lot of repair, but Michael and his son were a great help over the summer," Janna said. "I hope to have it all done by our wedding next June."

Knowing her take-charge, efficient sister, Leigh

had little doubt that she would reach her goal. Janna had never let anyone or anything stand in her way... not even her younger siblings.

Leigh only had to close her eyes to remember her terror and confusion on the night Janna had abruptly left the house at eighteen, never to return. Janna had escaped, while Tessa and Leigh had been left in what was probably the most dysfunctional family in the county.

Maybe all of them had grown up to be strong, independent women, but even now, there was a certain level of tension between them...an awkward distance that still had not been fully breached.

"Have you decided where you'll live?"

Janna tipped her head toward the private wing, where she, her daughter and Claire stayed. "Probably here, until Michael sells his house in town. Then we'll build close by."

A gray-haired couple in matching red flannel shirts strolled by arm in arm toward the guest dining room.

"Duty calls," Janna said, pulling her strawberry-blond hair into a ponytail with a rubber band that she'd had on her wrist. "Claire was back in her room, last I knew."

Leigh sighed, feeling as if she were heading toward a lion's den.

Janna gave her a knowing look. "She was cranky the last time you came out, but she's in a better mood today. Tessa took her to the home place for the weekend and that always makes her happy."

"It was always just about the ranch," Leigh said softly. "Never us."

"Though she single-handedly managed to succeed, even with three little girls and a lot of debt. Pretty amazing, when you think about it."

Leigh gave Janna a surprised glance. "You've sure changed."

"I've gotten older. A little wiser." Janna shrugged. "She and I aren't exactly best buddies, and I don't expect we ever will be. But things are going a little better now. And speaking of going, I better get over to the dining room before my customers starve."

"No problem. I'll bring her back in a couple hours." Leigh continued across the lobby to the door leading to the private wing, memories of Claire and Janna's arguments reverberating through her thoughts.

Claire had been hard. Critical. Demanding, of all her children. She'd distanced herself by asking them to call her by her given name once they'd left grade school.

Tessa had simply soldiered on at the ranch, but as a teenager Janna had gone through a rebellious phase and had stood her ground. Terrified by the arguments that had ensued, Leigh had tried hard to disappear into the woodwork and avoid any attention at all.

That Claire and Janna now managed to live under the same roof was surely a miracle, and an answer to heartfelt prayers. Now that she'd moved back, Leigh wanted to take on her fair share of their mother's supervision, but it wasn't going to be easy.

She found Claire in her room, sitting in a rocking chair facing the window with an unopened *Western Rancher* magazine in her lap. She didn't turn around when Leigh tapped lightly on the door frame and said hello.

"You're late."

"Sorry. I had an emergency come into the clinic this morning." Leigh walked into the room to stand in Claire's line of vision, waited a moment to see if she would ask about the emergency, then continued. "It was a baby llama—cutest little thing ever. Huge dark eyes. Long lashes."

Claire snorted. "Useless animals."

"Not in the Andes. And here, they can be wonderful guardians for a sheep herd. They—"

"I'm aware of that," Claire snapped.

Leigh took a deep breath. "So, are you ready?"

A brief flash of confusion crossed Claire's face.

"I'd like to show you the clinic. And my apartment, too. Maybe you can give me some ideas on what to do with it."

"On *decorating?*"

The derisive note in her mother's voice was unmistakable. "I'd just like you to see it. I wish it was bigger, so you could stay with me for a few months."

"I have a home. The main house, down at the

ranch." She waved a disparaging hand at her bedroom. "And that's where I ought to be, not here. Foolishness. Every bit of this situation is sheer foolishness."

If Janna thought this was a better mood, Leigh wasn't sure she wanted to be around for a bad one. "Well…would you like to go for a drive? We could take my truck out into the pastures to see how your cattle are doing, and we could go check on your brood mares."

Claire sniffed. "Tessa hasn't been here for days. You'd think she could find the time, but I suppose she's off on those pack trips of hers."

Apparently, that was an oblique form of agreement. "Let's go then. We'll look at your livestock, then maybe we can stop for lunch in Wolf Creek. I could still show you the clinic then, on our way back."

"I suppose we'd better, while it's still open."

"Still open?"

"Doc Adams was an institution around these parts. I doubt the ranchers around here will take kindly to some young gal trying to take his place." Claire stood, tossed her magazine on her bed and started for the door. "They won't believe you can do it, but you'll find that out soon enough."

Her mother's casual dismissal of her career bit deep—but after all her years of college, she hadn't expected anything less.

She'd been at the top of her class, won honors and scholarships, trying to prove to the world—and to herself that she could do this. But to Claire, she would always be the irresponsible daughter. The one who didn't follow through, didn't measure up. And with Claire's slowly advancing dementia, that probably wasn't ever going to change.

Leigh dredged up a smile. "Then I'll just have to prove those ranchers wrong. My first full day was yesterday and I already went out to—" She caught herself, belatedly realizing her error.

Maybe Claire showed signs of confusion at times, but now she jumped on Leigh's words without a flicker of hesitation. "Where?"

"Um…one of the ranches."

"Four Winds, I'll bet." Claire's voice grew flat. Cold. "You had no business there."

"It was a lameness exam, Claire."

"The buyer stole that place right out from under us. Conned Gray out of everything but his shirt."

"We don't know that for sure—"

"He *promised* he'd leave that property to me and my girls. Now ask yourself—why did he suddenly sell out, and where did all the money go? You stay away from there, you hear? Stay away!"

After several hours of jouncing around the Snow Canyon Ranch pastures in a pickup, looking at Claire's cattle and horses, they had a light lunch at the café in town, then Leigh turned up the highway and pulled to a stop behind the clinic.

"Would you like to see where I'm living? There's a small apartment in back."

Claire couldn't have looked less enthusiastic, but after a long pause she nodded and followed Leigh inside. She dutifully glanced in the tiny bedroom and combination living area and kitchen. "Not much space."

"But it's convenient, and it's clean. And it doesn't cost me extra to rent someplace else." Leigh shrugged. "With a little paint and some curtains it ought to work out for the first year, anyway. Want to see the clinic itself?"

"I'd like to go home. To…the lodge."

The defeat and sudden exhaustion in her eyes touched Leigh's heart. "Let me just check my mail."

She headed down the hall to the front entrance, where a small pile of envelopes lay beneath the letter drop in the door. She scooped it up and thumbed through the collection while she walked back.

Bills.

Credit-card applications.

Notices about some packages awaiting pickup down at the post office.

And a handwritten, plain white business envelope with no return address. Curious, she slid a fingernail under the flap and withdrew a single sheet of paper.

The words blurred, came into sharp focus, then sent a wave of shock through her. *Moving here will be a fatal mistake. Are you sure you want to stay?*

During the following week, the number of client appointments was lower than Leigh had expected. The week after that, there were fewer yet.

This week, she'd had farm calls for a sick goat. A cow with lacerations. A pony that had craftily managed to get into a grain supply and overindulge itself into a case of colic. In the clinic, there'd been a handful of clients each day. Not nearly enough— and she had loan payments due in eight days.

But what chilled her to the bone was the eerie sense that someone was watching her.

She'd started looking in her rearview mirror more often.

Checking the caller ID before picking up the phone.

She'd been leaving the lights blazing in the clinic at night, and more than once she'd stopped dead on the sidewalk in Wolf Creek and spun around—only to meet the startled gaze of some innocuous old duffer or a mom who'd abruptly gathered her children close to her side, clearly thinking *Leigh* was a threat.

And every time she thumbed through her latest mail delivery, she had to breathe slowly to calm her racing heart.

If someone was subtly trying to intimidate her, they were doing a good job of it, she thought grimly as she ushered a client into one of the exam rooms and lifted her Lhasa Apso onto the exam table.

"He's a perfect darling," Lois Bancroft breathed as she cradled the Lhasa's head between her manicured fingertips and met him nose to nose. "Just a wee bit spoiled, aren't you, baby?"

Leigh looked up at the starlet-thin woman standing on the other side of the table. "He's more than a little spoiled, ma'am. At this point, your dog is almost fifty percent overweight, and his adventures around town have given him a good case of fleas."

The woman's perfectly plucked eyebrows drew together in a frown as she glanced up at the vet-school diploma hanging on the wall, clearly doubting Leigh's professional skills. "You don't understand. Poor little Franklin *craves* adventure."

What the Lhasa needed was a more stable owner who could manage to keep him home and stop feeding him chocolates, but after three appointments in that many weeks, neither seemed to be happening.

"He needs to be kept in a fenced yard, Mrs. Bancroft, or taken for regular walks. On a *leash.*" Leigh tapped the dog's clinic file. "Otherwise, he might get hit on the highway or end up as a snack for some coyote. Then the least of his problems would be these fleas."

The woman leaned over to check her lipstick in

the shiny mirrored surface of the stainless-steel table. "I did have our yard fenced, Doctor. I'm sure Franklin just managed to slip out the gate." Her scarlet lips formed a moue of distaste. "It was probably the housekeeper's fault."

Leigh gently placed the dog back in its carrier, and pulled a couple of flea products from the shelves, including several aerosol cans of flea fogger. "You understand how to set these off, right? And how long you need to stay out of the house?"

The woman nodded.

"Good. Franklin's up-to-date on his shots, and his heartworm test is negative. Now that he's had his flea bath, he should be set. But he would be even better if you can help him lose five pounds."

"Sugar-free chocolates, then?"

A topic they'd discussed at every single appointment. Leigh fought the urge to roll her eyes and say something she would regret. "*None.* Chocolate is *toxic* to dogs."

Mrs. Bancroft drew herself up and sniffed. "You needn't be testy about it."

"I don't mean to be," Leigh said on a long sigh. "I'm just trying to make sure that he has a long and healthy life."

After the woman left, she sagged against the receptionist desk and stared at the stack of bills by the phone. She shivered despite the warm sunshine flooding through the windows.

Another slow month and her meager savings would be gone.

One more after that, and everything she'd worked so hard to achieve would be lost. And then, every prediction her mother had ever made about her would come true.

Oh, Uncle Gray...

At the sound of the bells over the front door, she glanced up with a big smile, ready to greet her next client—and found her sister Tessa standing in the entryway.

"I...need amoxicillin," she said, glancing at the empty waiting room. "For a calf."

No warm greeting, no sisterly hug, but either would have been completely unexpected. During the nine years Leigh had been away, there'd been little contact between them beyond occasional e-mails regarding family business, and perfunctory greetings during the rare occasions when they'd all been able to gather at Christmas. Claire's brand of mothering had left all of them with scars.

"No problem." Leigh managed a tentative smile. "Would you like a tour while you're here?"

Tessa gingerly stepped farther into the waiting room and looked around. "It looks like it always did."

"Believe me, I'm planning to make some changes. But first, I need to get on my feet, and that's going pretty slow." She followed Tessa's gaze to a faded Remington print on the wall. "I think that's been here for decades. I'm hoping someone can give me some ideas, because with all the wealthy people moving in from the West Coast, this place looks way too shabby."

"You're talking to the wrong person." Tessa snorted. "Janna might know about decorating. I spend most of my time on the back of a horse, remember?"

"You've got an exciting life, Tess. All those years I was in school, I can't tell you how much I envied you your freedom and adventures."

A shadow crossed Tessa's expression. "Right. Miss College Girl had reason to envy me. Look, I need to get going. Do you have that antibiotic?"

A promising moment of connection, lost thanks to the wrong choice of words. Longing curled around Leigh's heart for the love they'd never shared. For the bonds that had never really formed.

"I never realized it. You wanted to leave home, too," she said quietly. "I'm so sorry."

"Leave? I do what I want," Tessa retorted. "I'd go crazy, cooped up in a classroom day after day."

But before Tessa turned away, Leigh saw the truth in her eyes. The hurt and frustration at being trapped here in Wolf Creek—as the one left behind to take over the ranch, while her sisters went off to finish college degrees and Claire slipped into old age. And the fierce pride that would keep Tessa from ever admitting how she felt.

"You could still go back to school. Do something different."

"I made my choices. Maybe some were bad, but I'm doing what's right for me," Tessa snapped. "I'm happy. I have my own business. And I run the ranch as well as Claire ever did. So don't feel sorry for me."

Leigh brought a hundred-milliliter bottle of amoxicillin and a Ziploc bag of syringes and needles from the pharmacy. She handed them all to her sister. "I'm impressed by all you've done, Tess. And I never could've dealt with our mother as well as you have, either."

Tessa nodded curtly, started for the door, then turned back. "Did you ever find out anything more about that nasty letter?"

"Where did you hear about that?" Surprised, Leigh gripped the back of one of the chairs in the waiting room. But then she relaxed, as realization dawned. "I reported it to the sheriff's office, so I suppose Michael told Janna?"

"And Janna told me, the last time I went out there to pick up Claire. Has there been any more trouble?"

"Nope." Leigh swallowed hard. For the past three weeks, the incident hadn't been far from her thoughts. She still found herself wary of dark shadows, and held her breath every time she checked her mail. "Michael ran the fingerprints on the letter, but nothing came up in the system. After he recommended new locks and a caller ID on the clinic phone, I took care of both right away. But nothing else has happened since."

"Maybe it was just a stupid prank."

"Or the guy decided to back off. It probably helps that Michael sends one of his deputies cruising past here most every night, now."

"And word has probably spread that our future brother-in-law is the interim sheriff."

"Also very good."

"Still…" Tessa toyed with the bottle of antibiotics. "You should probably know that there are some rumors going around."

Leigh stilled. "Rumors?"

"I overheard them in the feed store, when Kent Miller didn't realize I was there. And at the drugstore, too." Tessa hesitated, her gaze fixed on her hands. "Folks are saying Doc Adams made a mistake selling his practice to someone straight out of school. They're saying you don't have skill or experience, and that you've already lost animals that would've survived if Adams was still here."

"I haven't lost *any* patients so far." Leigh strode to the windows, then spun on her heel and paced back again, helpless anger building fierce and hot in her chest. "I carried a 4.0 GPA throughout vet school, and spent an extra year doing an internship. During the past year I also worked nights and weekends at a hectic emergency clinic, where I got a lot of experience."

"If I were you, I'd want to know who's been starting the rumors, and why." Tessa shook her head in disgust. "Though I'd guess it's probably someone who's resented the McAllisters for a good long while."

"Which leaves a pretty long list."

"But neither of us can change the past." Tessa folded her arms. "You know as well as I do that Claire made an awful lot of enemies over the years. Remember what happened at the Bassetts' foreclosure sale?"

"Lonnie was in my class in high school. He was always giving me this eerie glare, and I know he's the one who trashed my locker." Leigh shivered at the recollection. "And his brother Trace was worse. He almost ran me off the road once."

Tessa nodded. "And remember when Claire evicted the Farleys from her rental property in town? They had three young kids, and I know they were poor."

"That was *awful*. I'm sure she had her reasons, but I was so embarrassed. I'll never forget the looks of condemnation we got from people we barely knew." Leigh stared at the empty chairs in the waiting room. "But we girls had nothing to do with it."

Tessa nodded, her expression reflecting Leigh's own feelings of frustration.

"So how do I fight something like this? I could lose the clinic if business doesn't pick up in a hurry."

For the first time, Tessa briefly touched Leigh's arm. "How bad is it?"

"Steadily worse since Labor Day weekend. I know most of the seasonal Wolf Creek residents pack up before Labor Day and some of the older locals go south. But still…"

The two sisters fell into awkward silence.

"Could you advertise?" Tessa ventured after a long pause.

"Guess what I tried wasn't very effective, if you didn't see it," Leigh said dryly. "I put some announcements about the clinic in the paper."

"How about local radio? Maybe you could do some five-minute 'Ask the Vet' spots on KTMV, just to get your name out there."

"The cost…"

"Hey, with a small station like that, it ought to be free—and you could show that you really know your stuff. Maybe they'll even 'pay' you by giving you some commercial airtime."

"Excellent idea!" Leigh fought the urge to pick up the phone this very moment. "Thanks!"

Pulling her truck keys out of a pocket, Tessa smiled grimly. "But don't forget about the troubles Janna faced when she moved home last spring. If someone has a serious agenda, they sure aren't going to stop with a few rumors or a letter. So watch your back."

THREE

On Wednesday, Leigh got called out to the Lazy B to pregnancy-check fifty replacement heifers and over a hundred cows. On Thursday, there were twelve paint colts to geld over at the Triple Bar in the next town.

On Friday, the phone didn't ring until three in the afternoon. At the sound of Brianna Daniels's young voice, Leigh turned away from her computer screen and grabbed a pencil.

"My dad's gone," the child whispered. "And I think my horse is sick. But Max doesn't think so."

"Can you call your dad?"

"I tried and tried." Brianna's voice rose. "But he didn't answer."

"He's got a cell phone with him?"

"That's what I tried," Brianna wailed. "I need you to come."

Leigh chewed the end of her pencil. "Maybe you'd better tell me about the horse, sweetie."

"He's out in his corral and he's all sweaty. He paws and he lies down, and then he gets up. A lot."

"For how long?"

"I dunno. After lunch sometime."

"Can I talk to Max?"

"He got mad about something, and he left. I don't know where he went." Brianna drew in a shuddering breath. "So maybe he won't even be back until later, and Polly doesn't know about horses."

"Polly?"

"She's our housekeeper."

"Can I talk to her?"

The phone clattered—perhaps dropped on a kitchen counter—and Leigh could hear the faint sound of Brianna's voice as she searched the house, calling the woman's name.

A minute later, Brianna returned breathless, sounding on the verge of tears. "I can't find her either. Please, can you come here?"

The child was there *alone?* What was Cole thinking, leaving his daughter with irresponsible people? "How old are you, sweetheart?"

"E-eleven."

Leigh asked for Cole's cell-phone number, and jotted it down. "I'll be there soon, sweetie. Don't worry. And stay out of Filbert's way, okay? If he goes down suddenly, you definitely don't want to be underneath him."

* * *

"No one called you," Max snarled when Leigh got out of her truck at the Four Winds Ranch.

"Actually, someone did," Leigh said as she pulled on her navy clinic coveralls over her jeans and T-shirt. She could smell the odor of beer on Max's breath from ten feet away, and from his surly demeanor, he was definitely a man who didn't like being caught hitting the bottle while on the job. "And I've left a couple of messages on Cole's cell phone, as well."

She walked past Max toward the sandy corral where Brianna was perched on the top rail of the fence. Today she was wearing jeans and pink cowboy boots, topped with a purple My Little Pony T-shirt. With a sprinkle of freckles over her nose and her gleaming brown hair in pigtails, she seemed too young and defenseless to be anywhere near a man like Max—especially without a parent nearby.

"How's your horse doing? Leigh called out as she approached. "Any better?"

Brianna's tear-streaked face didn't look promising, and when Leigh reached the corral, she could see that the child's fears were well-founded.

Filbert was lying flat, his coat wet with sweat, his sides heaving. He'd been thrashing long enough to dig deep, sweeping depressions in the sand. An empty water bucket lay on its side at the opposite corner, along wisps of bleached-out hay. Hay that had been tossed on the sandy ground, which was never a good idea. If it happened often, a horse could ingest enough sand to cause severe problems in the gut.

Max had followed her to the corral, and Leigh bit back a growl of anger when their eyes met. "You didn't want to call me? This horse sure looks colicky to me."

"He was just fine last time I looked." Max glared at Brianna and she shrank back, her face pale.

"You did the right thing, honey," Leigh said firmly. "I'll talk to your dad. By the way, did you ever find Polly?"

"Sh-she was hanging up laundry, out back." Brianna twisted a strand of her hair around her forefinger. "I couldn't find her at first, and I just got scared."

With good reason, if the poor child had to deal with someone like Max while her father was away— which was another topic Leigh planned to discuss, if and when Cole returned her calls.

She entered the corral and pulled on the old gelding's halter, urging him on until he finally staggered to his feet. Then she got to work, checking his temperature, respirations and pulse. Elevated to fifty beats per minute, his heart rate wasn't yet in the zone that predicted poor recovery, though his capillary refill time—checked by pressing a thumb against the pale gums just above his incisors—was just fair.

But when she listened for normal bowel sounds with a stethoscope held along his belly, they were almost nonexistent. Bad sign.

Most owners and stable hands helped during exams, by holding the horse's lead rope and murmuring words of encouragement to the suffering animal. Max stood outside the corral and watched, one boot hooked on the lowest plank of the fence.

"You didn't give this horse anything, did you?" She shot a quick glance at him as she searched through the leather bag she'd brought from her truck. "Home remedies? Colic preparations, Banamine or tranquilizers?"

"Nope."

"Good. You don't want to risk masking symptoms for the vet, and tranquilizers would be totally wrong anyway, but some people give them. How often has he been wormed?"

Max shrugged.

"You do know that putting his hay on sandy ground can lead to sand colic. Right?"

"I know my job, lady. I do what the boss says, and exactly that. No more, no less."

So Cole didn't see the value of a worming program, safe feeding practices or calling the vet when a horse was in trouble? What had happened to the boy he'd been in high school, when she'd seen him endlessly brushing his roping mare in the back lots of the various rodeo grounds? Talking to her. Stroking her neck, as if she were the most important thing in his life.

Though back then, with a wild dad like Rand Daniels, maybe that mare had been his one refuge.

After administering an analgesic, she performed a rectal exam, an abdominal tap to look for signs of rupture, then passed a nasogastric tube down Filbert's nose to check for fluid buildup in his stomach.

All the while, Brianna sat on the top rail with her arms wrapped around her stomach. Her eyes widened when Leigh asked Max to come into the corral to hold a gallon jug of mineral oil up high, while Leigh ran it down the tube.

"That looks *awful,*" Brianna whispered.

"He can't taste it, sweetie. The pain medicine is already making him feel better, and this is like a horse-size laxative. I think he's got an impaction in his gut, but luckily we've caught it before things got any worse."

The phone at Leigh's waist rang. Grabbing it with her free hand, she flipped it open when she saw Cole's number. "I'm at your place, but I'm a little busy—Filbert's colicking. Your daughter was in a panic about him, and she was right."

"Will he be okay?"

She ignored her unexpected sense of awareness at the sound of his voice. "Probably. Look, we need to talk." She glanced up and found Max staring at her, his eyes fierce and narrow. If he was worried about what she planned to say to his boss, he should be. "Can you call back in an hour or so?"

"I'm actually driving up Highway 49 right now—just passed Wolf Creek. I'll be home soon."

She clipped the phone back into its holder and gently withdrew the thin tube from Filbert's nose. "Can we turn him into the grassy lot over there?" She pointed to a small fenced pasture of maybe an acre. "He'll have more reason to move around in there, which will be better for him, and you can keep a close eye on what he does."

"That's where he lives most of the time anyway," Brianna said. She climbed down from the corral fence and opened the gate so Max could lead the gelding through. But she lingered next to Leigh and waited until Max was out of earshot. "You can stay, can't you? Just for a little while, to make sure Filbert is okay? Please?"

Looking down into her worried face, Leigh nodded. "Of course. I really need to talk to your daddy, anyway. It's no problem at all."

Leigh reorganized the supplies in the back of her truck while Brianna greeted her dad with a relieved hug. The two of them walked over to look at Filbert, Brianna chattering a mile a minute.

After Brianna scampered off to the house, Cole strode back to Leigh, his face devoid of emotion. "He looks fine."

Leigh scanned the surrounding building and corrals for Max, but he'd disappeared. "The horse was definitely going downhill by the time I got here. She wanted Max to call me, but he refused. She was pretty upset."

"Maybe he didn't think it was necessary."

"Filbert was sweating. In obvious pain and distress. Only a novice would think he was all right. Take a look at that little corral over there—you can still see the impressions where he was rolling."

Cole nodded, though she could still see a hint of suspicion in his eyes.

"Your horse could've twisted a gut, and then he would've needed surgery. Thanks to Brianna, we caught it in time."

Cole frowned. "Max worked on the Edwards' ranch for years."

"Well, I'm not so sure he's all that observant."

Cole glanced over his shoulder. Filbert was now dozing under a tree, his head and neck lowered and a hind foot cocked. The gelding was probably exhausted from its ordeal, but to a casual onlooker he simply looked relaxed.

Leigh could sense Cole's lingering doubt. "Look closer. You can still see the sweat marks on his neck and flanks." She shoved a clipboard into Cole's hands. "Take a look at his vitals, and read about what I did for him. He was one sick puppy when I arrived. Yet not only was Max irritated with me for showing up, but he seems to intimidate your daughter. And he also has…um…other problems."

Cole's brown eyes narrowed. "What?"

"Honestly, I think you should go talk to him right now, and see for yourself."

"Why?"

Leigh hesitated, uncomfortable with revealing something so negative about a person she barely knew, but even more uncomfortable with the fact a man like Max was responsible for Cole's livestock…and his daughter, if she happened to be around the barns. "I think he's been drinking, and I'm pretty sure he realized that I noticed. I also think he preferred sacrificing the horse to letting an adult catch him midday with alcohol on his breath."

Cole spun on his heel and glanced toward the barns. "Hold on," he snapped as he strode toward a cabin nestled behind a stand of pines, where Uncle Gray's ranch hands had always lived.

Did he believe her? Or was he planning to bring Max back for some sort of confrontation?

If he did, she would be ready to stand her ground. She'd done the right thing by speaking up, no matter what Max said. Though given the decades of bad blood between the Daniels and McAllister families, Cole might not see it that way. Years ago, he'd made it clear that he thought she'd lied on the witness stand at his father's trial. So why would he believe her now?

She winced at the vivid memories, slamming them back into the deepest recesses of her mind. She could only imagine how much her testimony had hurt him. And though she'd only spoken the truth, her feelings of guilt over his father's imprisonment had lingered in her heart ever since. She'd helped put the man behind bars…and in the process, had hurt his son.

The wonder of this whole situation now was that she and Cole had managed to be civil to each other…so far.

Glancing one last time at the neatly stored supplies in her vet box, she closed and locked the door. Waited a few more minutes. Checked her watch.

Maybe he wasn't even coming back.

With a sigh, she climbed behind the wheel of her truck and started the engine, then made a slow U-turn and started down the lane leading to the highway.

A second later, she saw Cole in her rearview mirror, waving at her to return.

She stopped, then backed up until she drew up next to him. "Well?"

A muscle ticked at the side of Cole's jaw. "He's gone."

"What do you mean, *gone?*"

"Gone. As in, his drawers are cleaned out." The anger in Cole's voice was palpable. "His closet is bare."

"I certainly didn't *tell* him to go, though frankly, it's probably good riddance."

Maybe Cole was upset with her, but she was no longer the shy, starry-eyed junior who'd fostered a hopeless crush on the coolest guy in the county, and she stood up for what was right. "If I found an employee drinking on the job, he'd be on the highway with his suitcase in five minutes flat." She shifted her truck into drive, but held her foot on the brake. "Even faster, if I caught him mismanaging my livestock, lying or intimidating my daughter. But that's your business, not mine."

"You think I don't feel the same way?"

Leigh thought about Filbert's thin frame and poorly trimmed feet, and realized that she knew very little about this man. "I honestly hope so."

Cole's mouth tightened. "I see."

"But I do understand that I wasn't called out here by an adult and that you have doubts about this farm call. So we can just forget about my bill. Fair enough?"

"No." He pulled his wallet from his hip pocket and pulled out three hundred-dollar bills.

When she didn't immediately accept them, he slipped them just inside her truck, on the dashboard. "This is on account, but send me a bill for the balance. Whether you want to believe it or not, I do pay my debts…and I won't accept charity from a McAllister."

* * *

Shifting his weight, a man hidden up on a ledge overlooking Four Winds Ranch cursed and repositioned his binoculars. He'd been watching the McAllister woman for weeks now, whenever he could. Keeping an eye on her activities. Planning his next move.

Today he'd followed her vet truck out into the country on yet another ranch call, and had felt his blood run cold when she'd ended up here—the last place he wanted her to be. His heart thundering in his ears, he'd found a good observation point, well out of sight.

Since then, he'd been purely miserable—the hot late-afternoon sun baking him from above; the rough granite ledge digging into his belly. He hadn't taken time to grab a water bottle from the truck he'd left hidden off the road a half mile back, but he hadn't dared go after it, either.

He'd watched. Waited. Felt his heart fall back into a steady rhythm when it had looked as if Leigh was done treating that scrawny old nag and would be leaving soon.

But then Cole Daniels's truck had pulled in a few minutes ago, and now he and McAllister were down there by the corrals, practically nose to nose. *Talking.*

The fact that both of them were suddenly back in Wyoming again had set up a gnawing pain in his gut the moment he'd heard the bad news. The fact that they were together, looking chummy, escalated that anxiety a hundredfold.

Uttering another raw curse, the man backhanded sweat out of his eyes and squinted through the binoculars once more, trying to decode their expressions, but the distance was too great.

Everything had been perfect, until now. Rand Daniels had been judged guilty. He'd conveniently died behind bars, precluding any risk that there might be some fool request for a retrial.

But his son was another story. A few years back, Cole had hired investigators to dig into the case. When they'd failed to find anything, Cole had hired yet another company...but they'd failed, too, thanks to some well-placed threats to the few locals who knew the truth.

And now Cole was back. *Permanently.* And given the rumors about him questioning townsfolk about the past, he was obviously still on his vendetta to prove his father's innocence. Still planning to stir up trouble.

And he would have all the time in the world to do it.

Worse, Leigh McAllister was here, too—the one witness who couldn't be controlled...unless she discovered that staying in Wolf Creek was too dangerous for her health.

Perhaps, it was time to make that clear.

FOUR

Cole appeared at the clinic the next morning. Surprised by the sound of his voice, Leigh leaned out of the surgery door for a second and motioned him to come on down the hall, then she ducked back in the room to continue suturing the Great Dane stretched out on the table.

She and Cole hadn't parted on the best of terms yesterday. But how could they? It certainly hadn't been a pleasant reunion of old friends. With such a difficult history between them, it was a wonder that they'd managed any conversation at all.

Cole was clearly still angry about his father's trial, and she certainly had reason to doubt the kind of man *he'd* become, given what Claire had said about the shady way he'd snared Four Winds. Was he really capable of taking advantage of a sick, elderly man, and taking the inheritance that should have gone to the McAllisters?

Yet she'd also felt a flare of her old, undeniable

attraction to him—as impossible now as it had been years ago.

She tied off another suture.

Cole appeared in the doorway. He glanced between her and the anesthetized dog, then lifted his gaze to meet hers. "How on earth did you wrestle that dog up on the table?"

"It wasn't easy. But now that you're here, I'd sure appreciate help getting her down." Leigh reached over to turn off the anesthesia, then bent closer and tied off a suture. "I'm nearly finished."

"Spay?"

"Nope. Newborn disposable diaper." At Cole's muffled laugh, Leigh felt some of her initial tension ease. "She ate it, the foolish dog. According to her records, she has also consumed a wallet, half a turkey carcass, and her owner's lingerie—all of which resulted in visits to Doc Adams. If she keeps it up, we'll have to consider installing a zipper on her belly." She completed another suture. "So, how can I help you?"

He silently watched her tie off the last four sutures. "I came to pay my bill."

"I don't have it figured out yet. I may even owe you money, if you overpaid." She checked the dog's cardiac rhythm and oxygenation on the monitor, then removed the patches and pushed the equipment cart aside. "I'll take her front end, if you can handle the hips." She tilted her head toward a soft bed of blankets she'd arranged next to the wall. "I want to move her over there so she'll be safe and comfortable while she wakes up."

He moved into position, waiting while Leigh lowered the table a few inches, then they gently transferred the dog to the blankets in one fluid motion.

"Thanks." She hunkered down by the dog and watched the steady rise and fall of the animal's rib cage. "Looking good, Dinah…till next time."

When the dog started to stir, she carefully removed the trach tube from its mouth and throat.

"I also came to apologize about Max's behavior toward you. Brianna said he was downright rude."

She rose and dropped the trach tube in a stainless-steel pan with her surgical instruments, then began collecting soiled gauze squares and bits of suture material for disposal, wrapped them in a wad of surgical drapes and dropped them in a red hazardous-waste bag. "Did he ever come back?"

"Hopefully he will, for his last paycheck." Cole shoved a weary hand through his hair. "He left a stash of empty whiskey bottles in his closet and a list of unfinished chores and projects a mile long."

"A model employee," she said dryly. "Lucky you."

"According to his past employers, he was a good one. But I need someone I can trust, and he was the wrong guy."

"I'm more concerned about your daughter. She seemed intimidated by him, and I don't blame her."

"She never said a word, but I wish she had." Cole's mouth flattened to a grim line. "It's hard enough for her as it is."

"With you being gone a lot?"

"That, and the move itself." He cleared his throat and glanced at his watch, obviously backtracking away from something too personal to share. "I… guess coming back here has been a little harder than I thought. On both of us."

Surprised, she studied him more closely and found shadows of pain and sadness in his eyes. And realized, with chagrin, that she'd never fully understood how tough his situation had been all those years ago. What would it be like, seeing your father convicted of murder and sent to prison, and then losing your home as well? Knowing it was all a constant source of whispers behind your back?

She'd said it long ago, but knew she needed to say it one more time. "I—I'm so sorry about what happened to your dad."

She expected that he might brush aside her sentiment, just as he had as an angry teenager. Instead, he pinned her with a searing look that seemed to freeze her in place. "He wasn't guilty."

"I remember so little about it. It's all a blur now. Like a bad dream."

"You don't remember?" A muscle ticked at the side of Cole's jaw. "You certainly didn't hesitate to go up on that witness stand."

Her heart faltered. "Gray spoke the truth, but he hated having any part in sending your dad to prison." She bit her lower lip. "And I was *subpoenaed.* I had no choice but to testify."

"Well, you were wrong," Cole said quietly. "My dad didn't kill anyone, and I plan to prove it."

But how could he ever disprove such blatant guilt? She tensed, driving away the familiar images of blood and death, and of seeing Rand Daniels standing over the body. She'd had nightmares for years afterward, and still felt unreasoning fear of the dark, and of enclosed spaces where someone could be lurking in the shadows. "I was there, Cole. Believe what you want, but I saw that knife in his hand."

The Great Dane twitched. Peddled its legs, then floundered into a half-sitting position, its eyes bleary and disoriented. She reached out to keep the animal from tipping over.

"There's no way I'll ever believe it." He headed toward the front door, reached for the knob then turned around to give her a cold glance. "And I promise you, I have all the time in the world to uncover the truth."

As a teenager, she'd had a secret crush on Cole— a handsome, self-assured teenager whose smoky-hazel eyes and careless grace had had every girl in the county dreaming about him.

Until the golden summer when she was fifteen,

she'd been too in awe of him to even speak. And then—wonder of wonders—they'd shared a growing, innocent infatuation. Banter. A single kiss that had stunned them both…

But that had been followed by the night when he'd embarrassed her, by standing her up at the town's Fourth of July celebration. And then days later, by the horrifying evening when she'd witnessed the murder.

She firmly reined in her old attraction to him. He'd practically accused her of lying on the witness stand, and apparently he hadn't noticed his poor old horse was turning into a rack of bones. That spoke more about his character than any winning smile or smooth words.

"I wish you well," she said as she turned away to write a note in the Great Dane's chart. "But you really ought to pay more attention to those horses of yours. Filbert is in terrible shape." She tried to keep the censure out of her voice, but neglect of any kind always made her furious. "A good horseman might come out to your ranch, see that gelding and just turn tail and leave."

Cole sighed heavily. "Brianna didn't tell you about him?"

"Just that he belongs to her." *Poor thing.*

"We've only had him and his buddies for a month. Brianna was heartbroken about leaving her school friends in California. She also kept talking about the horses at a stable where her mother took her for riding lessons. She cried. Pleaded. Said they were all going to die. I thought it was just her imagination until I found out that the stable had gone belly-up and the entire herd was being sent through a sales barn. None of them looked any better than Filbert. Most were at least fifteen-twenty years old."

Surprised, she stopped writing and looked up at Cole. "Which would mean they were destined for slaughter the minute they stepped into a sales ring. What happened?"

"There were a couple of other families who bid on the ones that looked healthier. Those horses ended up in good homes. I—" He cleared his throat. "I ended up with the other four."

"Four?" Chagrined, she stared at him, embarrassed over how she'd lit into him for taking such poor care of his livestock.

"Filbert, and a few of his stablemates. I brought the other three from California this past week, and they don't look much better than he does."

And all just to make his daughter happy. She felt warmth rise up her neck. "So…um…your stable is filling up pretty fast."

"Not with paying customers, but this was important to Brianna." He tipped his head in farewell. "Think about what I said, Leigh. Justice wasn't served when that jury found my father guilty. Maybe you could help me clear his name."

She watched him go, wondering which Cole Daniels was the real man. The one who'd broken her young heart, stolen an old man's ranch out from under him, and who still embraced unsupportable paranoia about the ill will of the people in Wolf Creek—or the loving father willing to rescue a herd of hay burners simply to make his daughter happy?

Even as a child, she'd heard whispers about the Daniels family—Rand, known for his hot temper, heavy drinking and wild Saturday-night brawls. His brothers, who were even worse. The name had been synonymous with trouble.

Maybe Cole had turned out to be a far better man, but the fact remained—she'd told the truth in court. How could he expect to find out anything different now?

On Thursday, Cole parked at the far end of the two-block business area of Wolf Creek, then sauntered slowly down the street, casually keeping watch for his quarry.

It certainly wasn't the town of his youth.

Empty storefronts and shabby, tumbledown mechanic shops had been replaced by quaint little shops geared for the wealthy patrons who were migrating here from the coast.

Flowers and antiques and specialty chocolates. A wicker-basket store—though how someone could make a go of selling baskets, he wasn't sure. A café emanated the aroma of rich coffee—locally blended, according to the sign in the window.

He walked past all of them without hesitation because these enterprises wouldn't draw the people he was after.

With Max gone and no replacement in sight, there was precious little time for anything but chores, but today he'd come into town early. In thirty minutes Brianna's school was over, and until then, he planned to start scouting out the possibilities for a little conversation.

Leigh was still sure his father had been guilty. There hadn't been so much as a flicker of doubt in those pretty green eyes of hers. A disappointing revelation because he'd hoped that she'd thought about it over the years, and had realized that she was no longer quite so sure about the "facts" that she'd recited on the witness stand.

Though maybe it was all the more frustrating because he still felt a simmering attraction to her, while she continued to stubbornly stand in the way of justice.

But *someone* in this town had to remember the night sixteen years ago when Wes Truly had been found dead outside the Hilltop Tavern on the edge of town. In a community this size, few skeletons stayed in closets—especially the most closely guarded kind.

Ahead, an American flag lifted gracefully on the

fitful September breeze high over the post office…
which was a definite possibility. He stepped inside
the tiny building—barely the size of a two-car
garage—and approached the silver-haired woman
behind the counter with an easy smile. "Would you
have some priority mailing supplies?"

She looked up. Squinted over the top of her half
glasses. He caught the slow dawn of recognition,
then the stiffening of her back as she straightened.
"Of course." She waved a hand toward the shelf
behind her. "Take your pick."

He pointed at a box, not caring which one he chose.

She silently pushed it across the counter at him.
Her features were muted with age and obesity, but her
voice helped him finally place her. "Mrs. Halloway?"

She nodded, her expression wary.

"Kyle's mom, right?"

She stepped back and fiddled with the keys
clipped to her belt, perhaps unconsciously savoring
the safety they represented. Maybe those keys kept
her locked behind the service counter, but anyone
under forty with an agenda could probably vault
over it without hesitation. Could she actually
imagine he was a *threat?*

"I'm—"

"I know who you are." She shot a nervous glance
toward the back of the post office. "We've got you
on the route, now. North on Highway 49."

He'd expected to be shunned by some of the

folks here. He hadn't expected fear. "I was one of Kyle's classmates, remember?" he said gently. "He and I were good friends in grade school."

Her head jerked in a single nod.

"Is he still around the area?"

"N-no…Billings." She swallowed. "But my older boy is real close by. He stops over all the time. Stays a lot of nights, too."

He chuckled, hoping to put her at ease. "That's great. Next time you see Kyle, let him know I'm back. I'd like to see him again."

She looked away.

His frustration grew. "It's great to be back here," he added gently, unwilling to give up just yet. "I was in real estate out in California, but I guess ranching is just in my blood. So…what do you think of the school system here? My little girl is in sixth grade, and she was pretty scared about making the move."

"My niece is a music teacher at the middle school." Mrs. Halloway's expression softened almost imperceptibly. "Mrs. Kelley."

"Brianna has music second hour and loves her," Cole exclaimed, relieved to find some common ground. "I understand she's the nicest teacher there. I can tell you, it's a relief to find my daughter happy with *some* aspect of our move."

A tentative smile deepened the crinkles framing the older woman's eyes.

He wanted to delve into her recollections about

the murder sixteen years ago and start collecting possible leads. But so far, he'd been met with caution or polite distance from every person he'd spoken to, so he was going to take it slow. Especially with a woman who should be a perfect source of information.

"I can't believe how things have changed around here," he mused. "All the stores…cafés…probably the people, too. Is Don Miller still around?"

She hesitated. "Lives out on Highway 12."

"And Gabe Brown?" Cole chuckled, as if reliving a fond memory. "He was quite a character last time I saw him."

"Had a heart attack, back in '05."

"No!" Cole shook his head. "That's just hard to believe."

"Oh, he's not dead. But he's in the nursing home over in Salt Grass, last I heard. None too happy about it, either."

"What about Ed Quinton? If I remember right, they were pals."

A faint hint of impatience flashed in her eyes. "Lives here in town. He's probably in the phone book, if you want his address."

Yes. He'd gotten what he needed, and he wouldn't push his luck any further just yet.

"Good seeing you again, ma'am." He grinned and turned for the door. "And tell your Mrs. Kelley that I appreciate her."

Out on the sidewalk, he casually continued on his way, his thoughts racing.

Were the people here so convinced of his father's guilt that they figured Cole was capable of the same violence? Or was someone spreading rumors, trying to make sure the old stories were revived?

It had to be the latter—someone who knew the truth and wanted it kept hidden, and that was the person Cole needed to find.

And Mrs. Halloway had just given him the perfect place to start looking.

Leigh was frightened. Alone in a dark forest where the trees loomed over her and scraggly branches reached down to tear at her clothes, winding thorny twigs in her hair and around her ankles when she tried to run. They twisted tighter. She couldn't move. And though she screamed, she couldn't hear her own voice. The dead silence of the forest mocked her fear, her futile effort to escape.

From out of the darkness a tall shape emerged. Huge, with a sinister, scarred face that glowed silver in the moonlight, revealing stained and broken teeth.

His voice was low. Evil. Carried the stench of rotting flesh.

He reached out to scrape a long, filthy fingernail down her cheek and blood welled up to drip onto her white cotton shirt. "You can't hide, little girl. I know who you are, and I know how to find you.

Maybe tomorrow night. Maybe next week. You open your mouth, and I promise you'll be the next to die…right after your sisters."

He laughed, then snaked a hand behind her neck and jerked her closer to him. "Tessa," he hissed. "Janna."

He savored their names like delicious candy. As if he would enjoy every moment of seeing them die.

Then as quickly as he'd appeared, he took a step back and his form seemed to dissipate into the mist.

Leigh sat up with a jerk, tangled in her sheets. Sweaty and cold, her heartbeat pounding in her ears, she fumbled for the bedside lamp and switched it on to chase away the eerie streaks of moonlight that danced through the wind-tossed branches just outside her window.

Since she'd first seen Cole again, memories of her fifteenth summer had been returning. And with them, the nightmares she'd left behind. *Please Lord—please, take away these bad dreams….*

The night of the murder, she and Uncle Gray had been traveling home from a livestock auction. He'd seen a familiar truck parked by the tavern in town, and had stopped to pay the owner for some cattle. Leigh had stayed inside Gray's truck with the doors locked for those few minutes….

And then, in a split second, her entire life had changed.

She bowed her head and spoke the comforting words of the Lord's Prayer, then prayed for the emotional healing of family. For her mother's health. And finally, for protection.

Because she no longer doubted that someone was silently watching her…and that someday, her nightmares wouldn't be just her imagination.

FIVE

Blearily peering at the digital clock by her bed, Leigh hung up the phone and thought about her friends back in vet school.

She was one of just seven—and the only woman— out of her entire class who had opted for a mixed large- and small-animal practice. The rest had gone into small animal, which meant more regular hours. Seeing pets in a clean, air-conditioned clinic environment, with all the necessary equipment at hand.

They would not be going out into the country at four on a rainy morning to deliver a foal.

She quickly donned her navy coveralls and pulled her ponytail through the back of a ball cap. She'd prayed so many times that she'd made the right career choice. A half hour later, as she pulled her truck to a stop out at the Lawson Ranch, and a sense of excitement and anticipation spread through her, she knew she was where she belonged.

A figure in an ankle-length yellow slicker moved

across the beam of her headlights, motioning her toward a small loafing shed. Grabbing the duffel bag she'd stocked with supplies, she hunched into her own slicker and splashed through standing water to the three-sided shed where—luckily—the mare was at least protected from the wind and rain.

A weathered, ageless woman was kneeling at the head of a bay mare lying flat on the ground, its sides heaving. The woman looked up to greet Leigh, her eyes widening as her worried gaze veered over to the man who'd led Leigh to the shed. "I thought you called Wolf Creek."

"Did." He tipped back the brim of his hat. He had to be in his late sixties, with leathered skin and a weary expression. "Got *her.*"

"But—"

His voice lowered, urgent and desperate. "I couldn't get anyone else."

Comforting words. Leigh stepped forward, glanced around the shed for any hazards, then pulled her stethoscope from her bag and listened to the mare's heart and lung sounds. "How long has she been in labor?"

"Had signs, late evening. Started pacing. Pawing. Didn't start in earnest until…" The man checked his watch. "Almost two hours ago."

Leigh frowned. "That's way too long. Is this her first?"

"Yep." The woman took a tight hold of the mare's

halter when Leigh pulled on a shoulder-length plastic glove and began an internal exam. "I'm Ann Lawson, by the way. And that's my husband, Ken."

Leigh managed a brief nod in greeting. "Usually one of the foal's body parts…" a powerful contraction fought her progress "…or the shoulders can't clear the pelvis. At this point, there's some concern for asphyxia."

The mare struggled to rise up into a sternal position, her legs beneath her. Then flopped back down with a groan.

This wasn't good. "I can feel a single foot. Not both—and I can't feel the nose." Leigh glanced toward the rafters, where one bulb cast a dim glow. "Can we get more light in here?"

"Other than a flashlight? No." Ann's face betrayed deep worry.

"How far is your main barn?"

"A half mile or more."

Leigh turned to Ken. "My keys are in the ignition. Bring my truck through the gate. Swing it around so we can use the headlights."

"The mud—"

"I don't care. You can always pull the truck out later. *Go.*" She turned back to the mare and reached inside her once again. Then held steady during the intense, squeezing pressure of the next contraction. Gently she repelled the foal between contractions to gain working space. *Please Lord, help and protect this foal and its mother. Help me save them both.*

Her face white, Ann stroked the mare's neck. "This mare means everything to us—we invested a lot of money in her. If we lose her, I don't know what we'll do."

The foal's leg twitched. "It's still alive, ma'am.... Wait! I've got the other foreleg."

But the leg was bent backward, effectively blocking the birth progress. Leigh carefully positioned it, then gritted her teeth as another contraction shuddered through the mare. Prayed that she could find the foal's head.

If the neck was bent around toward the foal's hips, it would still be a long struggle.... "I got it! I got the nose!"

From outside she heard her truck roar to life. The squeal of a pipe gate swinging open. A minute later, headlights flooded the little shed with blessed illumination.

She gently maneuvered the head into better position. The muscles of her arm were aching and trembling as she backed away to let nature proceed.

With the next contraction, the foal's front feet appeared, one slightly ahead of the other, then its nose. With two more powerful efforts by the mare, the foal slithered out onto the ground.

No clean bedding, here. No nice, fragrant straw, and the chill night would present even more dangers to the stressed little one. But it was breathing. *Thank you, God—for Your miracle of life!*

"It's a filly," the other woman breathed. "Oh, Ken—and we did get a paint baby after all!"

Sure enough, there was a splash of white on the side of the foal's belly, along with high white socks and a wide blaze. "Late in the year to foal," Leigh said. "She could have a tough winter."

"I know. We bought the mare at a sale down south, late last October. Had no idea she was bred at the time."

"We'll be keeping her up in the corrals by the barn all winter," her husband said. "I'm just hoping we can get the appropriate paperwork from the previous owner so we can register the foal."

The mare rested for a couple minutes, then staggered to her feet with a guttural groan and turned around to nose her wet baby, her ears flicking back and forth and her tail lashing.

After all the pain of a first birth, some maiden mares were frightened of their newcomer. Some showed disinterest and promptly rejected it. But this mare instinctively began licking and gently prodding her daughter with maternal curiosity.

Leigh stepped back a few feet, watching the bonding process, then went out to collect a couple of towels from the front seat of her truck. "It's wet and chilly," she said. "So hypothermia is a big risk right now. Can we close the mare in here for a few hours?"

Ken nodded and went outside to each front corner of the shed, and pulled two long stock gates so they met at the center of the opening.

Ann held the mare's halter while Leigh towel-dried the foal, treated the navel with antiseptic and checked its vitals.

Not long afterward, it began its awkward struggle to manipulate those impossibly long, gangly legs and stand up.

"So far, so good. But you're going to need to watch to make sure the placenta is expelled within a few hours, and also watch this little gal for signs of respiratory distress." Leigh picked up her gear. Glanced around to see if she'd forgotten anything. "And you need to bring in some water and hay. Dry bedding, if you have it—or just spread the hay. If you plan to rebreed the mare, I should probably come back in a day or so to infuse her with some antibiotics and make sure she didn't tear."

"I… We're real glad you could come out." Ken cleared his throat. "About what I said…"

Leigh smiled. "No problem."

"We're just used to Doc Adams," Ann added, faint color staining her weathered cheeks. "And we'd heard…" She made a flustered gesture with one hand.

"That I was right out of school?"

Ann's color deepened. "Right. But no matter what they're saying about you around town, I think you did a fine job."

A mixed compliment—one Leigh wanted to delve into. But the woman was already embarrassed, so she just smiled. "Anytime."

It took a couple tries with forward and reverse gear to pull away from the shed and make it out the pasture gate. Streaks of light were just beginning to show when she reached the clinic.

Her arm and shoulder muscles ached. She was cold and damp, and her long, hot shower felt like pure bliss. Afterward, she set the alarm clock for an hour of sleep, then drifted off into troubled dreams.

The call had been a success—one more chance to prove her worth. But it had also given her proof that her problems weren't over.

Whatever they're saying about you ran through her head like a continual litany…along with the two questions that she still couldn't answer.

Who was trying to ruin her future here…and why?

"Why can't we go riding?" Brianna folded her arms across her stomach, and her lower lip stuck out. "It's Saturday, and you *promised.*"

"I did promise, and we'll go. Just not yet." Leaning on the handle of his pitchfork, Cole tipped his head toward the wheelbarrow in the aisle. "Two or three more loads, and we can bed the stalls. And then we have to sweep the aisle, fill the water tanks in the corrals, and run to town for the vitamin supplements for your horses."

"I thought you were going to find another Max."

"Definitely not another Max," Cole muttered under his breath. The man had stopped by late last night, loudly demanding his final paycheck. It had been on Cole's desk for three days, but he hadn't known where to send it. Max had all but accused Cole of trying to cheat him.

"But—"

"I'm advertising for a new ranch hand, honey. As soon as we find the right person, I'll be a little less busy."

"Mom always took me shopping. We went to movies and stuff."

"This is a different life, sweetie. Just look around you—what do you see?"

"Horses. Barns. Mountains."

"It's *beautiful.* This is going to be a wonderful life for us both, you just wait and see. It'll take awhile to adjust. That's all."

Brianna's eyes widened and filled with sudden tears. She turned away.

Cole started toward her, then stopped. She'd lived with her mother since the divorce, and since then she'd learned to manipulate with tears and emotional outbursts. Where did he draw the line? How did he know when those tears were real and when they were fabricated?

Feeling as if he were out of his depth, he lifted another fork full of damp bedding into the wheelbarrow. But when he looked up and saw a single tear trail down her cheek, his heart clenched. *Please Lord, help me handle this the right way.* Setting aside the pitchfork, he went over to her and pulled her into a gentle embrace.

"I know it's hard," he said. "You've faced a lot of changes this past year. But I promise you, you're going to love this place." He smiled against her hair, remembering. "Did you know that when I was a boy your age, I visited this ranch once? I thought it was the most beautiful place in the whole world. I couldn't imagine living in a place like this. And just *look.*"

She burrowed against his chest, lifting her face enough to follow the direction he pointed at.

"This ranch has the most incredible view of the mountains. And look out over the pastures, honey—that's grass so rich and lush that your old horses will be fat and sassy in no time."

When she didn't answer, he lifted her chin with a forefinger and looked down into her tear-filled eyes. "I'm sorry that we can't go riding right now, but we will soon, okay?"

"It's n-not that." She pulled away and rubbed out her tears with the back of her wrist. "It's—" She inhaled a shaky breath and spun away. "It's nothing."

His heart heavy, he watched her run down the aisle of the barn and head across the parking area just outside toward the house. What did he know about being a single father to an eleven-year-old girl?

Sure, they'd once been a big, happy family. He'd been a good dad and a good husband—he'd thought—until the day four years ago when Alicia had announced that she wanted a divorce. She'd moved out soon afterward, claiming she needed her freedom, though she'd soon started dating a wealthy, silver-haired dentist.

No matter what Cole had said, no matter how much he'd tried, she'd never relented. He could only imagine what she'd said to Brianna because the child had been wary and distant with him ever since.

Even more challenging, Brianna had grown into an emotional and moody preteen who seemed to speak a different language.

The phone on his belt rang. He frowned at the unfamiliar number and name on the digital screen. A dim memory came back to him from his days growing up in Wolf Creek. He let the call roll over into voice mail, then waited a minute and listened to the message.

A man named Lowell Haskins had left his phone number, asking about the job listed in the paper.

Even as Cole's heart lifted at the possibility of finding someone to hire, this time he wasn't going to make another mistake. Though court records were public, not every troublemaker got that far into the system. Maybe the sheriff would have some insights.

Cole walked into the tack room and paged

through the phone book lying on a shelf, then dialed the non-emergency number for the county sheriff's office and left a message with the secretary.

The faint sound of whimpering drifted in the main door of the barn when he left the tack room. He pivoted toward the sound and found Brianna crouched with her back against the building and her arms wrapped around her upraised knees.

A sense of failure washed through him. "Hey Bree," he said, hunkering down next to her. He reached out, wanting to give her a hug, but she pulled away.

"Leave me alone." She averted her face.

"Please, tell me what's wrong."

Her whimpers escalated to tears. "Nothing."

He could face an angry stallion, or manage an irritated bull. He handled difficult situations with employees. But when facing his daughter's tears, he felt as helpless as a five-year-old. He rested one hand on her shoulder and felt a tremble work its way down her spine.

"I know I can't fix everything," he said. "But give me a chance."

"N-not this."

"When you were little, you thought I was your superhero…."

"Th—the people here sure don't think so." She sniffled.

Awareness dawned. "Is this something that's happening at school?"

She gave a jerky nod.

"Are the kids mean to you?"

She didn't answer.

"It can be really tough starting a new school, especially in a small town where everyone has known each other all their lives. Sometimes…they can say things that aren't nice."

She picked at a frayed thread on the knee of her jeans.

"I know it was tough when I had to change schools after my dad died. I was in high school, and by then everyone already has their best friends." He pulled her closer to him and draped his arm around her shoulders. "It won't be long, and you'll have lots of new friends."

She shook her head. "It isn't that."

He waited silently, encouraging her to continue.

"It's what they say about you." Her voice broke. "Terrible things. And about your dad, too."

He stilled, knowing what was coming next.

"Th-they say my grandpa was a murderer, and he deserved to die in prison. And th-they say everyone kn-knows you're just as bad." Her voice rose to a wail. "They don't even know you, and they say bad things like that."

"Honey—"

"I don't want to live here anymore," she cried. "I want to go back and live with Mom."

So now the old gossip had been resurrected, and had filtered into the middle school? He should have known it would happen. He'd been through it himself. In grade school and middle school—because kids picked up on what their parents said, and everyone knew about the wild Daniels family anyway.

In high school—after his father's trial—it had been nearly unbearable. Only a deep, ingrained sense of pride had kept him from running away, and the eventual move to his uncle's place in California had been an answer to his prayers.

He closed his eyes briefly. Tried to find the right words, and failed.

Coming back to Wolf Creek had given him a sense of closure on the past. It had represented victory over those who'd considered him just another worthless Daniels. But at what cost to his beloved daughter? He no longer cared about what anyone said about him—he was beyond all of that. But now *she* was facing senseless bullying.

He'd be visiting the school, and he would do everything in his power to make it stop, even if it took a lawyer to do it, but kids could be subtle. Sneaky. And still make her life unhappy.

Living here beneath the troubling specter of the past wasn't going to be easy for her, but there were even more painful issues that were beyond the law. Problems he couldn't fix.

Alicia had demanded the divorce, then had recently turned over their child's custody to Cole. "Mitchell wants to get married, but he doesn't care to go through the whole parenthood deal again," she'd announced. "And with grad school and all, I just don't have the time, anyway. It's your turn."

There was no way Brianna deserved to hear that she'd come in second to her mother's rich boyfriend. *Please Lord, help me say the right things to her—help me do the right things. I know I can't carry this on my own. I don't want her to be hurt like I was.*

Cole's cell phone rang and he automatically reached for it to mute the aggravating tone.

Brianna pulled away, glared at the phone, then stumbled to her feet. "See? You don't have any time for me, anyway. I want to go home!"

A guttural, agonized cry ripped through the air. Then whimpers, laced with terror. As if someone— or something—feared discovery, but was too frightened to stay silent.

Leigh jerked upright out of a sound sleep.

Her heart pounding, she gripped the edge of the blankets for a split second. A nightmare—or something real?

The heart-wrenching cries crescendoed. Unearthly sounds that made the hair stand up at the back of her neck and sent an icy shiver down her spine.

Something—likely a dog—was in terrible pain, and it sounded as if it was right outside her door.

She jerked on a pair of jeans and a sweatshirt, pocketed her cell phone and rushed to the back entrance, peering out into the predawn gloom.

A hunched figure slipped into the darkness beyond the reach of the security light.

Something was struggling on the ground just a few yards away, half-hidden by her pickup. She blinked, her breath catching in her throat. Then eased the back door open and scanned the parking area for any other sign of movement before taking a cautious step outside. "Hello? Is someone out here?"

There was only silence—save for the intermittent, agonized cries of the animal.

Down the road, a diesel truck motor roared to life. Tires squealed on pavement, probably in a hasty U-turn, and then the vehicle sped away.

Gripping her cell phone, she took another cautious step outside…and then her heart fell.

Someone had left an emaciated Border collie tied to the front bumper of her truck with a piece of twine. It cowered against the vehicle, looking up at her with crazed, white-rimmed eyes, its bared teeth gleaming in warning. A low growl rumbled from deep in its throat.

Its black-and-white coat was tangled and muddy;

its front left leg was heavily matted with blood and dangled at an impossible angle. "At least someone brought you here," she whispered softly. "So now, we just need to get you inside."

She glanced again at the dim shadows at the edge of the parking lot. Until this morning she'd felt safe at the clinic, with its good locks and sturdy doors. But someone had been at her back door, and she hadn't awakened until the dog had cried out.

If someone did have a vendetta against her, he could slip up to the building just as easily. He could smash a window to gain entrance before she could even call 911…and climb inside before help could possibly arrive.

All around her, the dusky shadows seemed to shift into threatening shapes.

Coalescing.

Looming closer.

Dispersing.

From somewhere far down the highway came the distant sound of an approaching vehicle. A loud diesel—all too similar to the one that had just left.

Her heart shifting into overdrive, she began sweet talking the dog toward tentative trust and prayed that she could get the animal to safety inside the clinic…

Because there was no way she wanted to be caught outside if that stranger was coming back.

SIX

With a compound, comminuted fracture of its foreleg and a damaged spleen, the Border collie's surgery had taken almost two hours, and then Leigh had stayed close by to monitor its stabilization and recovery.

Janna called right after church, her voice laced with worry over Leigh's absence, then she and her daughter stopped at the clinic afterward.

"Wow," Rylie breathed, staring at the dog sleeping in one of the four stainless-steel runs inside the clinic. "He's got a cast and everything! Does the needle hurt?"

"Maybe just a little pinch when I started his IV. He needs it for fluids and antibiotics right now." Leigh flicked a finger against the tubing, checking the drip rate, then studied the digital monitor screen. "He's lucky to be alive."

Janna frowned. "You have no idea who dropped him off?"

"None. Except that it was a diesel pickup, and the guy who did it was mighty sneaky." Leigh scooped her hair away from her face and sighed, the early morning's events now settling weariness deep into her bones. "I suspect the guy ran him over, and was decent enough to haul him here, but not honest enough to risk being seen. He was probably worried about being responsible for a big vet bill."

"So the dog didn't have a collar?"

"Nope."

"Did you let Michael know?"

Leigh shook her head. "Not yet, but I will. Maybe someone will call the sheriff's office about their missing dog."

"Poor thing." Janna lowered her voice. "Will he make it?"

"With his overall condition I didn't know if he'd survive the surgery." Leigh studied the dog through the bars of the cage. "He's so thin that he might've been a stray, and he lost quite a bit of blood from internal injuries. If he isn't a stray, then somebody ought to be held accountable for letting him starve."

"Can you keep him?" Rylie looked up, her eyes sparkling. "Or maybe we could!"

Janna chuckled. "I don't think so, honey," she said, ruffling her daughter's hair. "Ian and Michael are both talking about adopting a greyhound, and you already have a dog."

Rylie's face fell. "But what if he goes back to same bad place that had him before?"

"I'll make sure that doesn't happen," Leigh said firmly. "I'll be taking plenty of pictures of him to show the kind of shape he was in, when he first came here. And if I have to go to a judge, I'll do it." She tipped her head toward the hallway and led Janna to her office for a few moments of private conversation. "How's Claire doing?"

"About the same. She refused to come to church with us this morning, but I figured she wouldn't. Luckily, I still have Lauren working for me. Her family goes to Saturday-evening services, so she's able to cover the lodge for a few hours on Sunday mornings."

"I just wish I had room for Claire here, to give you a break. I know that a few afternoons a week don't help you all that much."

"But it does. She'd never admit it, but it's good for her to get away now and then—and a few hours are just about right. More than that, and she'd be worn out."

"It's different when she goes to Tessa's. From what she says, she could stay out at the ranch the rest of her life and be perfectly content."

"We've just got to do the best we can." Janna's voice was filled with empathy. "We'll never be Claire's first choice, but that's all right. I'm just thankful that Tessa was always here to help her."

Leigh studied her older sister's face for a long moment. "Do you realize what we've just done?"

Janna raised an eyebrow. "We agreed?"

"We've just had our first truly companionable conversation in *years.*"

By Monday night, the Border collie was eating and drinking, and Leigh was able to discontinue the IVs. By Wednesday, he was managing to hobble around the clinic on three legs.

Phone calls to the sheriff's office, other vet clinics in the area and a private humane shelter had yielded no leads regarding the dog's owners, and Leigh had succumbed to the gentle pleading in his beautiful eyes.

On Wednesday night, he slept next to Leigh's bed. By Thursday, he'd graduated to the covers at the foot of the bed, though Leigh had to help him up. And for the first time in almost a week she breathed easier as she settled under her blankets.

"If someone turns up and claims you, it'll break my heart," Leigh said, reaching out to stroke the dog's silky coat.

Resting his muzzle on his good front leg, the dog seemed to understand every word. In the faint moonlight that filtered through the curtains, she could see his golden-brown eyes, warm and watchful, as if he were guarding the most precious thing in his world.

But a split second later, he erupted into a frenzy

of barking as he awkwardly levered himself to his feet and turned to face the bedroom door.

Leigh's heart lodged in her throat amid the cacophony of barks and the flying bedcovers as the dog scrambled off the bed. Landing in an awkward heap, he yelped in pain, then managed to throw himself at the door.

This time, she didn't hesitate. With shaking fingers she punched in the speed dial for 911 and requested immediate assistance. Then she pulled on her clothes, grabbed her old shotgun from the top shelf of her closet and opened the door leading into the hallway.

The dog flew to the back entry and launched himself against the door with a resounding crash, falling in a heap once more—then he tried again, barking loud enough to wake the dead.

Maybe there was just a stray coyote outside. A few head of loose cattle. A client who hadn't thought to call before stopping in with a late-night emergency.

But over the past few days she'd had an eerie sense that someone was watching her ever closer, and this could be a late-night visitor of a far different kind.

And this time, she was going to be ready.

On Friday there was no school, and Cole had promised Brianna a trip up to Grand Teton National Park—with the condition that she first help him round up as many barn cats as they could find for a trip to the vet.

Now, he walked into the clinic with Brianna on his heels and four young cats yowling and thumping about in a dog-size pet carrier.

"They sure aren't happy," Brianna said darkly. "Maybe they'll be mad after this and just run away."

"If they do, at least they won't be creating lots and lots more cats."

"We could've had *one* more litter. To…um…help with the mice."

Laughing, he set the carrier on the floor. "There's at least three other cats on patrol in our barns that we couldn't catch. I think we're covered in the mouse department."

The front door had been unlocked and a bell had chimed when they'd walked in, but no one came out to the desk.

"Maybe she's gone," Brianna said hopefully. "We could just take our cats home."

"And try to catch them again? I'd bet it would be ten times harder the next time."

The back door slammed and voices filtered up the hall. A moment later Leigh appeared, followed by a tall, broad-shouldered man in a tan Jackson County Sheriff's Department uniform with Michael Robertson engraved on a silver name pin on the shirt pocket.

A ragged Border collie limped along behind them, one foreleg encased in a heavy cast.

"I'm so sorry I kept you waiting, Cole," Leigh murmured. Her voice was weary, and her smile didn't reach her eyes. She turned back to look up at Robertson. "Call me if you hear anything, okay?"

Michael nodded, then gave Cole a head-to-toe glance as if sizing him up and cataloging the data for future reference. "I don't believe we've met."

Cole extended his arm for a brief handshake. "Cole Daniels. I bought Four Winds."

Recognition, then chagrin flashed in the other man's eyes. "I was supposed to call you back about one of your job applicants. I'm afraid I didn't get the message until yesterday."

"No problem. Do you know anything about Haskins?"

Leigh drew in a breath. "*Haskins?* Isn't he—"

"He had nothing to do with your sister's problems, Leigh."

"But my mother…" Leigh fell silent, obviously torn about saying too much.

Michael rested a hand on her shoulder and met Cole's gaze. "Lowell worked for Claire McAllister awhile back, but she fired him after he allegedly got drunk and fought with another ranch hand. Since then he hasn't found steady work around here, and apparently he still blames her for that."

"So why doesn't he move on?"

"His disabled father lives at the old trailer park south of town. I tried to set Harvey up with county services, but he won't have a thing to do with the visiting nurses," Michael added with a hint of a smile. "Now that he knows I'm engaged to a McAllister, he's none too welcoming to me, either."

Cole frowned. "No one else has responded to my ads, but I don't want to borrow trouble. Not with a daughter at home."

"I did a background check on him. His legal record was clear…other than a disorderly conduct charge back in '89 and a couple of traffic tickets. Claire did make life harder for him, though, and her actions still stick in his craw."

Something that Cole could relate to, unfortunately. "So what's going on here?"

"Someone broke into Leigh's vet truck last night."

"After drugs?"

Michael looked down at the clipboard in his hand. "Everything they could find—though they didn't manage to open two of the compartments."

"They took syringes and a lot of medication. They also damaged some of the equipment." Leigh bit her lower lip. "The sheriff came right away last night, but we couldn't see the full extent until this morning."

"What they did to the truck itself was senseless," Michael added. "They destroyed hinges and locks on the compartment doors of the vet box, and smashed the heating and cooling compressor, too."

At the broken expression on Leigh's face, Cole suppressed an unexpected impulse to draw her into a comforting hug. "Are you insured?"

"Not well enough—the deductible is a thousand, and I'm not sure if the supplies are covered."

Michael's mouth flattened to a grim line as he sized up Cole once more. "I've dusted for prints, and I'm not closing this case until I find out who was responsible. One way or another, we're going to make sure there's full restitution."

Throughout the day in Grand Teton National Park, Cole mulled over Robertson's words. The unspoken message had come through just as clearly.

Cole had never had a juvenile record in this county or anywhere else. In California, he'd graduated summa cum laude with a business degree, and he'd built a successful company from the ground up.

Yet here—in the sidelong glances and whispers, and even the apparent assumptions of the sheriff—he was Rand Daniels's son once again; the son of a murderer. An outsider. Someone who looked like trouble and had the family genes to prove it. He'd made it through his last year of high school on sheer guts, masked with tough teenage bravado—distancing himself from his peers with cool disinterest.

Watching Brianna swim in the crystalline waters of Jenny Lake, his heart ached for her. As an adult, what others thought didn't concern him. Unless it hurt his business…or worse, hurt his daughter.

And that was exactly what was happening—

though he'd gone to town for a serious talk with the school administrators, and they'd promised swift and significant retribution to any child who violated the anti-bullying rules.

Had it been a mistake to come back? A decision based on some sort of subconscious vendetta over something he couldn't ever really change?

The memory of the last time he'd seen his father came back to him. The harsh antiseptic smell of that stark, windowless visiting area. The smudged wall of glass between inmates and visitors, with a row of plastic chairs on either side. The suffocating heat in the room on that oppressive July day.

His dad's face—sallow, drawn, defeated. "I didn't kill that man, son," he said. "I swear I didn't."

He'd said it at every visit. Cole had believed him then and believed him now—despite the almost irrefutable testimony of a number of witnesses who had been in the tavern that night.

On the way home, Cole took a detour down into Salt Grass and found the nursing home that Mrs. Halloway had mentioned.

It was a long, U-shaped building with white siding and blue shutters, and a wide, fenced lawn with benches and flowers to ensure that the residents didn't wander. The receptionist's face lit up when Cole asked about seeing Gabe Brown.

"Room 134, and he'll be thrilled," she gushed. "He hardly ever has any company. Are you a relative?"

"Friend." He surveyed the waiting area by her desk, then rested a hand on Brianna's shoulder. "It'll be boring for my daughter to listen to Gabe and I talk. Can she stay out here?"

"Of course! She can watch the television or go look at the birds in the aviary—it's right around the corner. I'll keep an eye on her, too." The receptionist pointed to a guest register on a nearby table. "Just make sure you sign in."

"Thanks." He gave Brianna's shoulder a quick squeeze, then jotted his name on the sheet and walked down the hall.

The blinds were drawn shut in Gabe's room, filtering prison bars of sunlight across the man's bed. He stirred, stared at Cole, then wrestled himself up in the bed. "Who are you?"

"A guy from the past," Cole said with a half smile.

Gabe's eyes narrowed. "If you're that new orderly, I ain't taking no bath."

The air in the room was dank with the scents of unwashed male and a faint hint of urine, and Cole guessed that the man was probably a big management problem for the staff.

"I'd definitely take that bath, if I were you. Don't want to offend all those pretty little nurses, do you?" Cole moved to the window and opened the blinds, flooding the room with harsh sunlight.

Holding his hand in front of his face, the man squinted against the light. "Get out."

"I'm just stopping for a visit, and I'll leave in a minute. But I have a few questions first. I'm Rand Daniels's son, Cole. Remember him?"

The old man sucked in a breath, his startled gaze riveted on Cole's face. His hand dropped to the bedcovers. "Why'd you come here?"

"I need to know about the night of Wes Truly's murder."

"I—told the sheriff everything I knew."

"I'd like to hear it again."

Gabe chewed on the inside of his cheek, his fingers twisting the hem of his bedspread. "Been too long. I don't remember."

"Try."

Gabe's left hand drifted over the call-button device lying on the bedspread. "What does it matter?"

Cole drew a chair next to the man's bed and settled into it with what he hoped was a friendly smile. "I was only sixteen when my dad was convicted. Ever since, I've believed the charges weren't true, so it would help me to hear about what happened. I know you were there that night. Playing poker at that table with my dad and the others."

Gabe scowled. "Lousy cheat."

"Who was?" Cole crossed a booted foot over the opposite thigh, making it clear that he wasn't leaving anytime soon.

Gabe flicked a nervous glance toward the open door to his room. "Shut that."

Cole complied, then returned to his chair. "Someone was cheating?"

"Wes Truly." Despite the passage of so many years, Gabe's voice filled with spite. "Drew us all in. Wiped us out. Don lost his mortgage money, and I—" He clamped his mouth shut and turned his face toward the wall.

"What?"

The man's neck turned ruddy. "I was engaged back then. Prettiest little gal ever. But she came looking for me, and said I'd promised to stop drinking and gambling. Told me to come with her right then—but I couldn't. I was too far in the hole. She left saying she'd never trust me again after that."

"So…both you and Don had reason to be furious at a weasel like Wes."

Gabe uttered a curse under his breath. "What do you think? But neither of us killed him."

"Who else was there?" Cole prodded gently. "Please—I was only a kid. I lost my dad over this and I'd just like to know."

Gabe closed his hand over the call-button cord.

"You, my dad, Wes Truly…" Cole prompted him.

The man's heavy sigh set off a fit of coughing— the wheezy, desperate sound of a lifelong smoker. "Don Miller and Ed Quinton. Satisfied?"

The names matched those in the report Cole had received from the county. "So…there was a fight."

Gabe swore again under his breath. "Ed was in big trouble. We all were. Wes started like an average player and then took us for everything we had. Ed exploded—he figured the guy had marked cards, and someone in the room was spotting our hands for him. Crowded place like that, it's hard to tell."

"What happened, exactly?"

"The usual. A shoving match, then an all-out brawl. We weren't the only guys mad—some other guys dropped out of the game early."

"And then?"

"Bartender cut the lights. Ordered everyone to settle down or he'd be calling the sheriff. A bunch of us walked out and found Wes on the ground and your dad with a knife."

All of that had been in the report, too, more or less. But not what Cole needed most.

"You mentioned there were others...some who'd pulled out of the game earlier."

Gabe flicked a nervous glance at Cole, then pinned his gaze on the opposite wall. "It was dark and smoky in there. Crowded. How would I know?"

"One name."

"No idea. *Now get out of here.* Understand?"

"Please?"

He pressed the call button and reached up to rest a hand on his chest. "Chest... My chest hurts."

"The staff doesn't always come right away, I'll bet." Cole frowned. "I'll go get help."

"You do that." Gabe's voice was low and hard, not the weak effort of a man in severe pain. "And don't come back."

SEVEN

Janna and Michael stopped by the clinic Saturday morning to invite Leigh out to the lodge for dinner. The invitation could've been extended by phone, but she suspected they were mostly concerned about how she was handling things after the vandalism on her truck. Touched by their concern, she reassured them both that all was well. But it wasn't.

Tessa called less than an hour later, ostensibly to ask about cattle vaccines, though from her oblique questions, it was pretty clear that she'd heard about what had happened.

Leigh finally gave in. "You must have talked to Janna."

"Well…yes."

"I suppose she told you about what happened to my vet truck."

"Of all the rotten luck. Did you lose a lot of expensive stuff?"

Leigh closed her eyes. "Enough."

"But it isn't just the money, I'll bet," Tessa retorted. "It's creepy, just knowing someone trespassed on your property."

"Exactly. I expected to feel safe here. I remember unlocked doors and everyone knowing everyone else. But now…I'm no longer sure."

"If…um…you need a place to stay for a while, you're welcome at the ranch. I know it's too far away and inconvenient, but…" Tessa fell silent for a moment. "Well, you used to have all those nightmares, and I know you didn't like being alone. After that Daniels incident, I mean."

Leigh wasn't about to admit the nightmares were back to the older sister who'd always been so strong and determined, even in the face of her own tragedy at nineteen. Tessa had refused sympathy then, and it had been an unspoken topic ever since. And she still never let anything stand in her way. "I slept with the lights on for years—until one of my college roommates put her foot down." Leigh smiled into the phone. "Thanks for the offer, though."

"Janna said there was a lot of damage to your truck."

Leigh gratefully grabbed the abrupt change of topic. "Just the vet box in back. Someone took special care to damage the heating and cooling system—almost as if he knew that would be worse than just stealing."

"Teenage vandals are like that," Tessa said bitterly. "You can only hope the little monsters are caught and have to pay up."

Had it been teens? The various possibilities had been running through Leigh's thoughts all day. Growing up in Wolf Creek, she'd never had any enemies to speak of, but her mother sure had. Could someone be out to revenge against anyone with the McAllister name?

Michael hadn't sounded worried about Lowell, but if he was such an innocent guy, why had Michael investigated him when someone had started harassing Janna last spring? And then there was Max—who'd simply disappeared after being caught drinking on the job. Did he carry a grudge over that?

"Leigh? Are you still there?"

"Sorry. I was just thinking about who the vandal could be. And now, I've got to figure out how to maintain the proper temperature for my vaccines and antibiotics when I'm out on calls. It's going to be tricky, this time of year."

"No kidding."

They both fell silent for a moment. A cooler and ice packs might do the trick on warm days, but October was just two weeks away, and there'd already been snow on the higher ranges. Freezing temperatures would soon be reaching this lower elevation.

"Have you gotten any estimates yet?"

"I called a dozen places yesterday and this

morning. I found one mechanic in Salt Grass who could do the repairs, but he can't fit me in until the end of next week. And that's just if the parts arrive by then."

"I… Well, maybe we haven't always gotten along in the past, but I just wanted you to know I was sorry to hear about all of this. See you at Janna's tonight for supper?"

Warmed at the unexpected words, Leigh smiled. In time, maybe they would finally be able to share a closer relationship than ever before—something she had prayed for many times. "I'll be there, barring emergency calls."

But as soon as Leigh hung up the phone, the enormity of the situation at the clinic settled back on her shoulders like a blanket of iron.

The truck could be fixed.

The missing and damaged equipment was being replaced—there'd been no option.

But all the expense and aggravation was starting to get to her.

With a sigh, she double checked all of the locks on her vet truck, then started through the clinic to make sure every window and door was locked as well.

The injured Border collie hobbled along behind her every step of the way. She smiled down at him, then dropped to one knee and hugged his neck. "No word yet on who you are," she said. "Maybe you'll get to stay. In the meantime, we should give you a name," she murmured. "Fred? Spot?" She thought for a minute. "Hobo?"

The dog licked her cheek and leaned into her, and she laughed. "Hobo it is."

At the sound of tires on the gravel outside, he stiffened and pulled back; his ears pricked and a low growl rumbled in his throat.

A thread of anxiety slipped through her as she rose and looked out the waiting-room windows. She'd parked out in front after coming back from a farm call, and her own truck was the only one out there. Whoever had come, they'd parked out of sight around the building.

But for as long as she could remember—clear back to her childhood—the clinic had always closed at noon on Saturdays. All the locals knew that—and the big sign out at the road listed the hours, too.

Sensing her wariness, Hobo awkwardly struggled to his feet and moved to her side with his hackles raised as she strode down the hall, glancing out the windows in the first and second exam rooms along the way.

A moment later, the back door squealed open and a figure appeared in the doorway, silhouetted by the sunshine behind him.

Hobo's brave stance melted in the face of an actual confrontation. Whining, he drew back behind Leigh's legs.

"Some watchdog you've got there."

"Neil?" Relief rushed through her at his familiar face. "What are you doing here?"

"You didn't hear me drive up?" He snorted. "Gotta say, you're gonna be in big trouble if the wrong person comes along. You should have the back door *locked*."

His supercilious tone rankled. "I was just in the process of locking up—and I was headed that way."

"During the day, you should always have it locked. You being alone here and all." He shook his head, as if she'd committed a truly stupid error. "Don't you think?"

She silently counted to ten, then added a prayer for patience. "I usually do. I just took some trash outside, and—" She stopped, inwardly chastising herself for making excuses. He had no business questioning her. And he shouldn't have waltzed right on in as if he owned the place, either. "Is there something you need?"

He came down the hall, peering into each room. "I heard about your trouble."

Stunned, she stared at him as he passed her on his way to the reception area. *"How?"*

"Common knowledge, sugar."

"B-but you're clear over in Salt Grass."

"I have a police scanner." He braced an elbow on the tall counter and leisurely perused the desk and credenza. "Everyone listens to the county 911 calls around here. Believe me, everyone. Best way to keep up on what's going on."

She glanced pointedly at the desk, then met his gaze straight on. "Well, everything is fine here. So if that's all…"

"Are you in a hurry to leave?" He checked his watch. "I figured you would be closed by now, and would have time to talk."

"About what?"

His smile was overly gentle and patient. "You know as well as I do that business hasn't been the same since my uncle left. I worry about you trying to hang on too long, then losing your shirt over this deal."

"That isn't going to happen."

"Oh, it will. And it won't take long. I know the McAllister pride is an issue here, but no one needs to know that you couldn't make it on your own. Look, this practice has already devalued. Word gets out, you know. How much confidence are the locals going to have in you?"

She felt her blood chill. If Neil wanted her practice, just how far would he go? Was he behind all of her problems? "Their confidence will be *growing*. I'm already getting more calls, and success is the best advertisement, don't you think?"

His mouth twisted in a faint smirk. "Glad to hear you think it's going well. But consider what I said. I'm looking into buying a second practice in the area, and if I find a better one, I won't be interested in yours. You'll lose your best shot at partnering with a strong practice like mine."

News that wouldn't break her heart. "Don't count on hearing from me, Neil. But thanks for your interest."

He shrugged and walked out the back door. She followed him, and locked it firmly behind him.

Irritating man.

Irritating, *presumptuous* man.

She stared out the window and watched him leave, a ripple of uncertainty working its way through her stomach as his truck disappeared.

Someone was spreading rumors.

Someone who had easy access to pets and livestock owners. Was it Neil? And would he go as far as breaking into her truck, just to make her life more difficult?

She eyed the countertop where he'd rested his hand.

Fingerprints.

Would they match those on the vet equipment that had been tossed to the ground outside her truck? Would there be prints on the damaged compressor?

With a grim smile, she picked up the phone.

He hadn't planned on the dog.

Sure, he'd expected some vet patients locked away

in the clinic's kennels. But not a crazy, vicious animal ready to tear down that back door and come after him the night he'd wanted to break into the vet clinic.

He kicked at the crate of pharmaceutical supplies and surgical equipment that he'd managed to grab out of Leigh's truck. And then, after taking a hard look around him, he shoved it all over the lip of a ravine. At the sound of shattering glass, he smiled. It was the sound of money. A *lot* of money.

He'd planned on a whole lot more that night. Something...personal. Memorable. His smile settled into a satisfied smirk at the thought.

Quite possibly, something exquisitely painful.

But there'd be another place. Another time. And when he was through with Leigh McAllister, she'd be high-tailing it out of Jackson County, and she *definitely* wouldn't be coming back.

Not if she valued her life.

EIGHT

Leigh spayed and vaccinated Cole's barn cats on Saturday, then waited for Michael to stop back and lift Neil's fingerprints from the countertop.

By Monday morning, the cats were doing fine and Michael was at the clinic with disappointing news.

"No match on the prints," he said. "All I found was your prints—and a couple of faint ones from Doc Adams."

He looked tall, dark and imposing in his sheriff's uniform, and she knew Neil would already be sitting in the county jail if there'd been a match. Michael was one of the nicest men she'd ever met, but he took his job seriously and she'd seen tough-looking cowboys give him wide berth.

"If it was Neil Adams, I'd bet he wore surgical gloves," she grumbled. "He's *such* a detail-oriented guy."

Michael reached down to scratch Hobo behind the ears. "Has he been back?"

Leigh shook her head. "I think he believes I'll be calling him any day now, to tell him that the clinic is in deep trouble. That's why I wondered about the fingerprints. He sure seems to have a motive."

"You'd also mentioned a guy named Max. The one who used to work out at Four Winds Ranch."

"He probably blames me for losing his job out there, but the funny thing is—he didn't get fired. He just walked off. He could've stayed and explained himself. Maybe even kept his job."

"Unless he knew his boss well enough to figure it was a lost cause. I've asked around town about him, but no one has seen him since he picked up his last paycheck out at the ranch, and that was over two weeks ago."

"So he probably left the area, then."

"Maybe. I ran into Lowell Haskins at the gas station last night, and asked him about what he'd been up to lately. Just friendly questions, nothing more than that."

"And?"

"He says he's been helping his dad manage the trailer park. They're out at the old one, south of town." Michael frowned. "I know he's rough around the edges, and I know what your mother thinks of him. But far as I can see, he hasn't been in any trouble since the day she fired him."

"I don't know anything about him. He worked for her after I went away to school, and I just vaguely remember hearing his name when I was a kid. A lot of the ranch hands don't get to town much, and I sure didn't, either. You think he's a safe bet as an employee for Cole?"

The radio speaker clipped at Michael's shoulder erupted with a burst of static, then a rapid-fire message from a dispatcher regarding a domestic disturbance.

He pressed a button on the mic. "On my way." He gave Leigh an apologetic look. "Sorry, I've got to go. As far as Lowell is concerned, I only know that I didn't find anything on him in the county court records."

"Cole and his daughter ought to be here any minute to pick up their cats. I just wasn't sure what to say if he asked me about Lowell."

The clinic phone rang minutes after Michael left, and a local rancher asked about having his calves castrated. She set up the appointment for the next day at 10:00 a.m., then went back to the pharmacy and began stocking a cooler with the antibiotics and vaccines she would need for her afternoon trip out to a hobby farm north of town, where the owner kept a pet llama and a few dozen sheep.

When the bells over the door jangled in the waiting area, she went back out front and found Cole at the desk with Brianna at his side—and felt her heart skip a beat.

Since Friday, she'd been thinking way too much

about him. Little things—like his slow, deep voice, that sent ripples of awareness through her. The loving way he'd kept a hand on his daughter's shoulder, as if silently promising that she didn't need to worry—that he would always keep her safe.

Without a father in her life, Leigh had always been drawn to men who were good and nurturing parents. Had always felt a tug at her heart when she saw what she'd longed for as a child. Who would've guessed that the son of wild Rand Daniels would have turned out so well?

Years ago, Claire had endlessly railed against that "no-account" family, and when she'd suspected that Leigh was attracted to Cole, she'd turn livid. She'd predicted that he'd be a brawler and a drunkard like his daddy. Guaranteed that he'd end up in prison, too, since he was growing up with a dad like Rand and had no momma to lead him down the right path.

But she'd been wrong.

"Are the cats done?" The girl's eyes sparkled as she peered around Leigh to look down the hall. "Can I see them?"

"Of course. I'll bet you'd like to see the other animals, too." Leigh looked up at Cole. "If you have time."

He nodded. "Bree tells me that she'd like to be a vet when she grows up."

"She's welcome at the clinic any time, if she'd

like to see what I do. You can even drop her off for an afternoon, but you'd better call first."

The girl's eyes rounded with delight. "Awesome!"

Cole laughed. "I guess that's your answer, right there."

Leigh led the way down the hall to the kennel room, where banks of stainless-steel cages lined two walls. She lifted Cole's portable kennel onto the counter, then loaded the cats inside, one by one.

"You'll need to bring them back in ten days so I can remove the stitches." She gestured toward the other cages. "You're welcome to look, but don't put your fingers through the bars. You never know—even a gentle dog is stressed in this environment, and can be unpredictable."

Brianna's expression melted as she slowly walked past all of the cages. Suddenly she stopped and knelt in front of a cage of mixed-breed puppies. "Ooooh! They are so sweet—but where's the mom?"

Leigh slid a look in Cole's direction, and knew exactly what he was thinking. In about five seconds, his daughter was going to be begging him for at least one of the occupants of that cage, and he was already trying to figure out how to say no.

But brave man that he was, he didn't try to hurry his daughter away, and that raised him another notch higher in Leigh's book.

"I'm afraid the mother died," Leigh said. "She was a farm dog and was hit by a pickup. The owners didn't know what to do, so they brought the puppies here this morning."

"Awwwwww." Brianna pressed closer to the cage. "How old are they?"

"About four weeks, so now I've got them on re-placement formula. They should do well, though. They seem to be pretty healthy."

Brianna looked over her shoulder at her dad, her eyes shiny with tears. "That's so sad. Isn't it? I bet they miss their mom a whole lot."

Just as Brianna probably missed her own mother, every single day.

Cole cleared his throat. "But this is the best place in the world for them right now, with good vet care."

"But—"

"What would poor Sammy do if you brought home a puppy?"

"They'd be friends?"

"No matter, those pups are way too young to be given away. They really need to socialize with each other."

"I could take care of them," she wheedled. "I *promise.*"

"Every few hours around the clock? That's a big responsibility."

"But I can come back to visit?"

"Definitely, sweetheart."

As his daughter chattered on about the puppies, Cole angled a meaningful glance at Leigh. At his almost imperceptible nod, she knew he'd be letting Brianna select a puppy later. Not just because he would be caving in to her pleas, but for far deeper reasons.

Leigh wondered about the absent Mrs. Daniels, and guessed that there'd been a painful divorce that had left the little girl feeling bereft. *I've come here to live with my daughter,* he'd told Leigh during her first vet call at his ranch.

Brianna's sudden switch of topics jerked Leigh's attention back to the present.

"…and maybe you and Mom can take me to Florida this winter. Wouldn't that be fun? And then…"

At the grim set of Cole's mouth, Leigh guessed there weren't going to be any fun, family trips for them in the future.

Cole murmured something that made Brianna turn away in a huff, but a moment later the child rallied.

"Maybe Dr. McAllister could come out and go trail riding with us sometime?"

Embarrassed by Brianna's innocent question, Leigh busied herself with checking all of the cage latches. Today's conversation with Cole had been less awkward than usual, but she had no doubts about his disinterest in reviving any sort of friendship with a McAllister—and definitely not with her, the one who had helped destroy his family.

"That sounds good," he said smoothly. "But right now we'd better get going, honey. We've got to get your cats back home, and then I've got some guys coming out for interviews."

Leigh lifted an eyebrow. "Interviews?"

"Two, actually. Haskins and one other guy. I've also gotten calls from three or four others." Cole shrugged. "From what I can gather, Haskins mainly had issues with your family. Other than that, his record is pretty clear."

"R-r-right." She knew the doubt in her voice spoke volumes, but could she honestly give a specific instance of anything the man had done? Her knowledge was hearsay, gleaned from a mother who tended to aggravate people, find fault in them and make enemies, and that was hardly fair.

And Claire had certainly been wrong about Cole.

He and his daughter made it to the front door before Brianna stopped and tugged on his sleeve. "What about *today?*"

"What?"

"Can she come out today?"

A corner of his mouth lifted in a wry smile. "I'm sure Dr. McAllister has a full day ahead of her."

The hero worship in her eyes was unmistakable when the child looked back at Leigh. "We could have a trail ride and a cookout and—"

Cole hesitated, then shook his head. "She's a busy lady, Brianna."

Leigh took pity on him for the difficult position he was in—trying to be polite, but surely wanting to avoid such an awkward social commitment. "Maybe another time."

But then Cole met Leigh's eyes, and even before he spoke, she knew he was only trying to make his daughter happy. "Actually, that sounds like a great idea," he said. "Are you free on Saturday?"

Cole smiled to himself as he and Brianna walked out to his truck.

Leigh had stilled after his invitation, clearly on the verge of declining, so he'd added casually, "Brianna would love it. I get the feeling she admires you quite a lot, and I can ask you about some of the guys who've been applying for the job at my ranch."

At his daughter's whoops of delight, Leigh had agreed, but with a tentative, weary expression that told him exactly how thrilled she was.

Too bad.

Maybe with some gentle nudging she could recall the night of the murder, but through the filter of an adult viewpoint, after all these years. Maybe she'd seen something—or someone—out of place. Heard something that had seemed inconsequential back then, but that could be a significant piece of evidence.

Though, if he were going to be completely honest with himself, the thought of spending time with her also brought back happier memories—those brief, golden moments when he'd sensed her interest, and had imagined a future with her at his side.

He and Leigh had never gotten that far, of course.

As kids they'd seen each other at livestock auctions, rodeos and horse shows for years. She'd grown from a sweet little imp to a petite, determined dynamo with the prettiest green eyes he'd ever seen. But she'd always been under the protective wing of her uncle Gray or her vigilant, marine sergeant of a mother, and she'd been nearly unapproachable to a kid like him.

Until she'd come up to him one day, a blush staining her cheeks pink, to shyly stammer out a question about an upcoming rodeo. She was fifteen, a year younger than him. And he'd fallen hopelessly, helplessly in love with her on the spot.

After that, they'd hung out together at the rodeos. Shared some stolen moments away from the crowds.

A single kiss.

Until Claire McAllister and her brother Gray had apparently gotten wind of the situation and cornered him one night out behind the chutes. They'd made their opinions crystal clear to the boy from the wrong side of the tracks with a rowdy father who couldn't keep out of trouble: stay away from Leigh, or the powerful McAllisters would find subtle ways to make sure Cole and his father paid dearly. And Cole had believed them.

The humiliation of that confrontation had stayed with him for years.

But now, he and Leigh were adults. Claire no

longer had that ultimate power and Gray was gone. So with luck and patience, Cole would soon be able to find out what Leigh knew about the murder…and there might be others in town who knew something, too. It would all just be a matter of time.

Brianna's voice pulled him back into the present. "We can really go on a trail ride? And have a cookout? You *promise?*"

"I promise, honey. I'll have Polly buy some good rib-eye steaks, and we can grill outside when we get back from our ride." He started up the truck. "Hey, as long as we're here in town, I should stop back at the nursing home and ask Mr. Brown another question. It won't take long, I promise."

Brianna rummaged through the purple backpack she'd left on the floor of the truck, then pulled out a book. "That's okay, this time I have something to do."

He eyed the book in her hands. "I thought you'd read that one already."

"I did, but the rest of my books are back in my room at Mom's house."

"Then, young lady, we definitely have to get you to the library as soon as possible. What do you think of that?"

She beamed at him. "Awesome!"

He suddenly realized just how quiet and isolated her life was, now that she was living with him at the ranch, and he felt a pang of guilt, followed by a sense of helplessness. How did one go about finding companions for little girls? And what did any of them like to do for fun? He didn't have a clue, and suddenly he felt out of his depth.

Back in California, kids joined Little League or soccer, and it seemed as if all of them took swimming lessons. But Wolf Creek just offered a small town square with some play equipment, and not much else.

He turned to her once he'd pulled to a stop at the care center. "Are you lonely, Brianna? Are you happy here at all, or is there something I should be doing better?"

Her answering smile wobbled at the corners. "I've got Sammy, and the horses, and my books. And I've got you, Daddy."

"But…?"

She ran a finger around the binding of her book. "I just want you and Mom and me to live together again," she whispered.

A rock the size of Texas settled in the pit of his stomach. Apparently Alicia had never bothered to fully explain the situation—preferring misconceptions to the awkwardness of trying to make things clear for her little girl. "You do know that your mom has a new friend. Right?"

Brianna nodded.

"And that Mom likes him whole lot?" Cole hesitated, trying to find the right words. "She might even marry him someday."

"No, she won't." Brianna's lower lip stuck out, much as it had when she was a little girl and stubbornly wanted her own way. "He's too old, and I don't like him. He's not like you."

This was not going well. "Look, let's just run inside quick so I can talk to that man, and then we'll go home. Okay?" *And when we get there, I'll be calling your mother for some advice and assistance.*

Brianna silently trailed along behind him, her book clutched to her chest.

As before, the bubbly receptionist was seated at the desk. He nodded to her and went to sign the guest book.

"Uh, sir…" This time, the receptionist's voice was subdued. "Can I ask who you've come to see? Was it Mr. Brown?"

Cole nodded, sensing bad news.

"I thought I remembered you from last Friday. He… He passed away that night." She offered a sad smile of condolence. "I'm sorry."

Cole stared at her. "He said something about his heart. Was it a heart attack?"

She gave a delicate shrug. "That's what the doctor thought."

"He doesn't know for sure?"

"*She* didn't order an autopsy, far as I know, and I handle the medical records here. If someone's under a doctor's care in a nursing home and has a chronic illness, there usually isn't one. Not in this county, anyway."

Warning bells sounded in Cole's head. Gabe had seemed nervous. Edgy. He'd insisted on having the door shut before he would say a word. Why, if Cole's questions only concerned a crime from long ago?

Suddenly, the true cause of death seemed important. "Did he have any family?"

"Nope. Sometimes I help contact distant family members, but there wasn't anyone. He hadn't agreed to a power of attorney, either—he was still making his own decisions, right to the end."

"Could you tell me the name of Gabe's doctor?"

"I—" She frowned. "I don't know. Privacy laws, and all that. Just wait a minute, okay?"

"Yeah." He joined Brianna by the oversize saltwater fish tank on the opposite wall. "It won't be much longer, sweetheart. The lady is just checking on something for me."

She looked up at him, her eyes rounded. "Did that man *die?*" she whispered.

"I'm afraid he did, honey. He wasn't in good health." Though he'd seemed like a tough old bird during that visit.

If anything, Cole had been fairly certain that Gabe had simply wanted him out of that room as soon as possible. But why?

At the sound of footsteps, he turned around.

"I checked with our administrator. She said I could tell you that it was Dr. Lohman who took care of Gabe. But that's all I can tell you. If you have further questions maybe you should call the doctor."

"Thanks, I appreciate that. Is she local?"

"There are no local doctors in this town," the woman said with a wry smile. "We're lucky that she comes here twice a week. Her office is in Salt Grass."

"You've been a great help. Thanks."

Cole walked with Brianna out to his truck, lost in thought.

Coming back to Wyoming had reawakened all the emotions he'd felt the night of his father's arrest. The fear and grief the day Rand had been sentenced. The numb disbelief when the police had knocked on Cole's college dormitory door two years later to say that his father was dead.

Now, someone was harassing Leigh. Was that somehow tied into the fact that she had testified at the trial? Was someone afraid that new evidence might surface?

The answers were buried here in Wolf Creek, and Cole had only begun to dig. And he was determined to find out who really killed Wes Truly.

NINE

Leigh eyed the two-year-old llama on the other side of the fence, then turned to the shaken owner standing next to him. For a man who easily topped three hundred pounds, Walt Fisher could run and scramble over a fence remarkably fast.

The woolly animal stood with its head high and ears pinned back, worked its jaws, then lobbed a wad of spit across the fence, issuing a challenge as clear as the animal's charge a minute earlier. The smelly glob fell just short of Walt's feet.

"Friendly," Leigh remarked.

"He was, as a baby." Walt shook his head. "He was an orphan, and my wife just fell in love with him at an auction. Had to have him. She bottle-fed him, and he was like a puppy, following us around the barnyard, cute as a button. And now—well, frankly, she's afraid to go in the pasture to check our sheep, and even I think twice."

"With good reason. An aggressive male can

knock somebody flat. I've seen owners with back injuries and broken bones."

Walt chewed on his lower lip. "My neighbors think I ought to just put Dagwood down before he sends one of us to the hospital."

"Most llamas are sweet and gentle, but this can happen with males handled a lot as crias. Especially if they were bottle-fed. They grow up thinking people are their peers, and have little respect. We need to geld him, and his sharp fighting teeth should be erupted by now. They need to come out as soon as possible."

"Maybe it's just not worth it even trying."

"I think it is, since he hasn't been used for breeding yet. Then I'd suggest you contact the llama breeder over in Carson. He keeps a herd of males pastured together, and maybe you can board Dagwood over there for a month or two." Leigh smiled grimly, remembering the aggressive posturing of the males that went on in that herd. The minute the owner haltered one of them for a health exam, at least three others had charged at it, taking advantage of its more vulnerable state. "Believe me, if there's any hope at all, those big boys will teach him basic respect. After that, you'll have a better chance."

After completing Dagwood's surgery and leaving him in a slightly woozy state, Leigh finished up the rest of her ranch calls and headed back to the clinic. Hobo, who had begged to come along using his irresistible, pleading expression, inched across the seat of the truck and nudged his nose under her elbow to beg for affection.

"Life is good, isn't it?" she murmured, rubbing him behind the ears. "I just need to keep busy, and this will all work out."

At the clinic, she pulled up to the back door and lifted Hobo out, mindful of his cast. Instantly, a medley of barks, loud meows and squawks erupted from inside the building, its open windows amplifying the noise.

"Well, everyone inside is sure happy to see us," she said, waiting for Hobo to do his business on the grass. She reached for the back door to usher him inside.

The doorknob turned too easily in her hand.

Which was odd because she never left the building without carefully locking every door.

Hobo whined and danced backward away from the entrance.

"Silly dog, you—" And then she looked down.

A dark apron of water was spreading out on the concrete.

She stared at her feet, then pulled the door open, and a torrent of water gushed over her boots. There had to be at least six inches of standing water in the hallway—and from the lab and exam rooms came the rushing sound of…*rain?*

Hurriedly, she tied Hobo to the front bumper of

her truck, then ran inside the building. Water poured from the sprinkler system in every room. Soaking equipment. Files.

She spun around and flipped off the main power switch and the water supply.

She splashed down the hallway to the front desk, where the counters were soaked, and all the file drawers were pulled partway out, to catch the water like mouths opened to summer rain.

Drips from the sprinklers splashed in the standing water, the staccato beat marking the ruin of almost everything in the building.

Water trailed down the pine paneling, which was already buckling in places. Cascaded in miniature waterfalls out of the glass-front cupboards in the lab. Pooled in the centrifuge.

In the kennel room, all of the cages held standing water. Dogs cowered at the back of their cages. Wet, irritated cats lifted one paw after another, shaking off the water in disgust.

The puppies were huddled together squirming and crying, clearly stressed and cold.

Grabbing the only dry towels she could find, she quickly wiped out empty cages, dried off the animals and shifted them into their new homes, one by one.

She held the puppies a while longer, wrapped in towels, rubbing them to stimulate their circulation.

How could this have happened?

Unable to quite take it all in, she put the puppies

in a dry cage, then went back down the hall and sagged against the door to her office. She stared at the soggy mess on her desk. *Dear Lord, I don't even know where to begin. Please, help me figure out what to do—because right now, my entire career is in ruins.*

The letter had seemed like an innocuous threat.

Her uneasy feeling of being watched could've been her imagination.

But the vandalism on her truck was a true act of aggression, and the likelihood that this was simple sprinkler-system malfunction was zero to none. In the back bathroom, hidden inside the vanity cupboard, she'd also found a broken pipe pouring water onto the floor. There was no way the dents and fresh scrapes on the pipe could have been accidental.

Somebody had been here. Somebody determined to cause even greater harm. And this time, he'd managed to cause almost irreparable damage.

She resolutely pulled her cell phone from the clip on her belt and called 911.

Michael, Janna and Rylie appeared within an hour, armed with two Shop-Vacs, mops and stacks of dry towels. When most of the water was mopped up, Michael brought in three industrial fans from an equipment rental place in town.

By early evening they all sank into the wooden chairs in the waiting room. Already, the building smelled musty; the water-streaked pictures on the walls were buckling inside their frames.

"It isn't just the cleanup," Leigh said. "An electrician will need to go through this whole building—and I'll bet he finds a lot of old wiring, in addition to the water damage." She glanced around at the plaster walls in the office area, which were now crumbling near the baseboards. "And I'll bet the walls in the waiting room are all like that, beneath the paneling."

"But you have insurance, right?" Janna rolled the stiffness out of her shoulders. "Won't that cover everything?"

"It's complicated. I'm in the process of leasing with the intent to buy, but Doc Adams agreed to pay the insurance on the building for the first year. The deal was that I'd find a bank to finance the rest of the purchase price at the end of twelve months, and then take over the insurance. If this building isn't salvageable, he and I will need to talk."

Michael frowned. "But insurance would cover the building, wouldn't it? That's the whole point."

"I just hope it's insured well enough. If it is, no problem. If it isn't—I don't know what I'll do." Leigh took a deep breath. "Even if he has excellent insurance, how long will it take to get somebody in here to repair this place, much less to do the work? I'll bet we're talking months. Many months."

"And your equipment?"

"Insured...but with a high deductible. *Again.*"

Janna leaned over and rested a hand on Leigh's knee. "In the meantime, you're welcome to use some space out at the lodge. You could have one of the cabins, plus the double garage or the barn. Whatever it takes to get you back on your feet."

Leigh leaned over to give her a big hug. "That is so sweet of you."

It was sweet, but impractical. There were twenty miles of circuitous, challenging mountain road between Snow Canyon Lodge and Wolf Creek. Miles that would discourage a good share of her walk-in business, and that would also place her at the outside edge of her busiest area for ranch calls.

But anything else in town—if there was even any usable space available—would mean paying rent in addition to her lease commitment to Doc Adams. And she still had the dogs and cats to consider. Some she could discharge a little early. But where would she kennel the others? And what about the pups, who needed to be fed around the clock?

Janna pulled back and studied her face with an expression of concern. "But it doesn't really help you, does it?" she said finally. "We're just too far away."

Leigh nodded, feeling numb. "If only…" She paused, realizing how truly selfish her words would sound. "If only Gray were still here. He had such plans."

"He did." Janna's eyes widened. "He'd talked

about your clinic for the last two years. Do you suppose…"

"He told me that one of his small buildings was perfect for a clinic. It was on some property he'd purchased next to his ranch, but with the lay of the land, it was a much shorter drive from town."

"Did he start remodeling the place?"

"He asked lots of questions about what I'd like in a clinic, but he wanted to surprise me. Last fall, he had a contractor get started. But then Gray passed away and the ranch was sold."

Janna's eyes took on an excited gleam. "I saw the exterior once. It's in a perfect location. Easy access to the highway, less than ten miles out of town. You think Cole has any use for it?"

"I have no idea. Michael?"

He thought for a minute, then shook his head. "Those buildings aren't in view of the highway, so I haven't noticed if there's been any activity. It sure wouldn't hurt to ask."

It sounded almost too good to be true—especially if the plumbing and wiring had already been done. But even if it was available, the rental could still be well beyond her means. And using facilities on Cole's land would mean encountering him far more often.

She knew that he probably still held her partly accountable for his father's death…and though it was illogical to feel guilt over telling the truth at the trial, she hadn't been able to let go of her remorse, either. Coupled with the confusing mix of emotions she felt about Cole, close proximity could lead to a very awkward situation.

Then again, she might not have to impose for all that long. Especially if the clinic could be repaired without too much delay.

After a swift, heartfelt prayer for guidance, she tried for a smile, though she knew it wasn't very convincing. "You're probably right. Even if a crew could start working on this damage tomorrow, it's going to take a long while for them to finish. And in the meantime, I need a place for my patients."

She pulled her cell phone out and flipped it open, then searched through its call history list until she found Cole's cell phone number. He answered on the third ring.

"It's Leigh," she said. "And have I got a proposition for you."

The Brownley place had last been used as a hundred-acre hobby farm for a couple of retired city folks from San Francisco—the last remaining relatives of the settlers who'd lived on the land back in the early 1800s. They'd knocked down the crumbling buildings and built a thirty-by-forty insulated, heated barn as a combination hobby shop and stable for a horse and a few goats. They'd added a small cabin for their own use.

But after one Wyoming winter, they'd packed up and moved back to sunny San Francisco, and Gray had eagerly snapped up the property, since his ranch surrounded it on three sides.

Leigh breathed a sigh of relief as she, Janna, Riley and Michael moved the last of the cages into the little barn. "The rest can wait until tomorrow," she said on a long sigh. "I can't thank you two enough!"

"Not a problem." Michael walked the perimeter of the barn, then checked out the cabin one more time. "Everything looks good and tight, and you do have your cell phone. But are you sure you want to stay out here tonight?"

"I have to. The puppies need watching, and I have a dog on IVs that I want to keep an eye on." She glanced at her watch. "Anyway, Cole said he'd be back home by nine tonight, and he would check in on me."

"I could stay with you," Janna said. She glanced at the dense pines that rimmed the little clearing. "You might like some company."

Leigh shook her head. "That's really nice, but you've got to worry about Claire and your daughter, and you've got all of those lodge guests, too. I'll be fine, and you'll be just a phone call away, anyhow."

"And I'll be sure to send a deputy cruising out here a couple times during the night," Michael added. "Have you talked to Doc Adams yet?"

"I left a message on his cell phone." She chuckled. "I imagine he is off having fun with all those other retirees and doesn't check his phone all that often. But really, I'll be fine right here once I get my equipment set up. I told Cole that I would barter veterinary services for the use of his building, and pay the balance in cash. He said I could stay as long as I needed to."

Michael jangled a set of keys in his hand. "I'm going to go over the clinic inch by inch, to see if I can find any sign of an intruder. We're going to get to the bottom of this, Leigh. I promise you that."

She waved at them as they drove off, then went back to the barn and started unpacking some of the boxes in the hobby-shop area. It was spacious, with counters and cupboards on all sides and vinyl flooring. Fluorescent light fixtures had been hung overhead, providing good illumination.

Hobo watched her from the blanket she'd folded for him by the door.

"So what do you think, buddy? Looks plenty good to me."

In an hour, she'd managed to unpack and shelve supplies, then went back to the kennel area and checked on her patients.

Apparently all of them had survived the stress of their unexpected, chilly drenching, even the litter of puppies and her one surgery patient from this morning, for which she was grateful. At least so far, none of them were showing labored breathing or an unexpected rise in temperature.

With a last glance at the cages, she whistled to Hobo and headed for the cabin where she'd dropped her suitcase, a hastily packed bag of toiletries, and the groceries that had survived the water sprinklers. The shadows had lengthened, and now the western sky had faded to indigo with faint streaks of lavender and rose behind the silhouette of the mountain peaks.

She and Hobo would be safe here.

Absolutely no one knew they'd come here, except for Cole, Michael, Riley and Janna…and the deputy who would be charged with keeping an eye on the place.

But that would soon change.

She had a vet clinic to run. Clients would be bringing animals here for treatment or boarding; the mail carrier would know, and soon the word would spread. A sense of unease skittered through her stomach and started tying it into a knot.

It just made no sense. She wasn't a threat to anyone; she hadn't caused anyone harm by coming here. The only person who seemed to openly resent her was Neil, but would he really go this far?

She pulled open the door of the cabin and helped Hobo maneuver up the stairs.

Then she turned and took a long, sweeping glance around the perimeter of the clearing.

In the soft light of early dusk, with Michael and Janna here, it had seemed like a pleasant, welcoming little place, the last of the fall wildflowers bobbing and dipping with a light breeze. Now, the deepening shadows seemed to hold secrets and silent threats that hadn't been there before.

She studied each shadow. Listened.

She heard nothing, save for the sound of a passing car and a distant owl. *"I know You're with me, Lord,"* she whispered. *"I know I'm safe in Your care. Please continue to watch over me and my family and friends, and all whom I hold dear."*

A warm sense of reassurance washed through her as she stepped inside the cabin and locked the door. Everything would be okay.

Everything.

At least until her unseen enemy knew she was here.

TEN

If he'd planned it, things couldn't have worked out better.

Cole headed up Highway 49 out of Wolf Creek, checking the odometer when he passed the city-limits sign. Though the two properties were now combined, the turn-off for the old Brownley place was almost five miles before the main entrance to Four Winds Ranch, due to several deep valleys and the circuitous mountain roads.

In the daylight, the road was easy enough to see. But now, on this moonless night, the usual landmarks would be hidden in the darkness.

He wondered if Leigh was nervously pacing the confines of that cabin, frightened by the isolation and the late hour, or if she'd simply gone to sleep. His ex-wife, Alicia, would have lasted about five minutes before climbing in her car and heading for a hotel room, but then she'd been raised a city girl, and Leigh was made of sterner stuff.

If it took promising that he would install a security system, hire a guard or rent her a pit bull, he'd do whatever it took to make Leigh feel comfortable on his property.

Because he wanted to keep her close by...at least until he'd had a chance to uncover everything she could possibly remember about the past. And in the meantime, he needed to carefully ignore his growing attraction to her. An attraction with the power to tie his gut in knots, because it went against everything he'd thought about the McAllisters for over sixteen years.

He'd dwelled on the lies he'd heard in court.

The ultimate price his own father had paid for the McAllisters' brand of honesty.

Yet, at every turn, he found Leigh to be the same sweet, straightforward gal she'd been as a teenager. His conflicting impressions of her were at constant odds. Perhaps she was too sweet and trusting for her own good, while he'd allowed himself to sink into bitterness and anger.

Cole hadn't spent a lot of time talking to God since his father's incarceration. As a teenager, he'd blamed God and the judge and the sheriff, and every last person in town for what had happened.

But lashing out at everyone and everything had been a poor coping mechanism back then, and it certainly wasn't any better now. He took a deep breath. *Dear Lord...I need to put all of these feel-*

ings to rest—please, guide me. Help me discover the truth—even if it isn't what I want to hear. I'm not getting anywhere with this, and I need Your help.

The miles of asphalt disappeared beneath the wheels of his truck as the road began to climb. Now, the tang of sagebrush and cattle gave way to the clean scent of pine, sharp and pure, and a sense of peace settled over him. The answers were here somewhere, waiting to be uncovered. And with prayer and persistence, he was going to find them.

He checked the odometer and slowed, then caught sight of the dusty road leading off the highway into the trees on the left side. He turned and kept the truck at a slow crawl up the rutted, narrow lane. Around the final bend, the trees gave way to a small meadow where all of the cabin windows glowed with welcoming light.

After making a quick call on his cell phone to identify himself, he jogged up to the door and knocked. A furious volley of barking burst through the door, coupled with the mad scrabbling of claws against the wood. Then he could hear Leigh settle the dog before the door opened.

She was backlit by the soft golden light inside, her strawberry-blond hair hanging long and loose. There must've been a candle burning on the counter somewhere behind her because the light seemed to dance and shift, setting off gleaming sparkles in her hair and scenting the air with cinnamon.

She looked impossibly delicate. Fragile. And once again, he wished he'd been able to convince her that she should stay at his house rather than out here all alone. But he'd already sensed that she'd grown into one of the most independent and stubborn women he'd ever met.

"You must be exhausted," she said, her voice husky and low. "Long day?"

"Enough." He looked past her. "Is everything all right? Electricity, water, gas?"

"Good to go." She tipped her head toward the interior of the cabin. "I'm afraid I've still got quite a jumble of boxes in here, but did you want to come in?"

He did, but there'd be another day and time, and he didn't want her to misinterpret either his reasons for offering the buildings, or for stopping by tonight.

"My other offer still stands," he reminded her. "There are two guest rooms up at the house, and both my housekeeper and Brianna are there so you wouldn't need to feel uncomfortable."

She tipped her head toward something leaning against the counter. A long barrel of a rifle, he realized.

"I'll let you know later, but tonight I think I'm perfectly fine."

"My house and barns are over five miles away on the highway, because of the terrain. But they're less than a mile as the crow flies, if you hike or ride cross country. If you were to honk your truck's horn, we'd probably hear it."

"I'm not worried. I spent a lot of my childhood here…." Her voice trailed off and she looked away, a shadow of grief in her eyes. "I know the area pretty well."

"I imagine you do." And she'd expected that she and her sisters would inherit it.

An awkward pause lengthened between them while he searched for the right way to respond.

She lifted a shoulder in a faint shrug. "If my uncle hadn't sold it to you, it would've been someone else, I guess. I suppose you must've felt a bit of vindication, over buying out the man who testified against your dad."

He felt a flash of guilt. "It wasn't my purpose in buying the place."

"Just a little bonus, right?" She gave him a weary smile. "Look, I know you blame my uncle and me for everything that happened, but we had no vested interest in seeing your father convicted of that crime."

"Except for that lifelong rivalry between my dad and your uncle."

"You think that Gray perjured himself on the witness stand over that?" She snorted in disbelief. "Why would he risk facing charges himself? For that matter, why would I?"

"A good question," he shot back. "Because that trial destroyed my family, and sent an innocent man to prison."

"You can't accept that we told the truth?"

"I…." he searched her face, looking for a flicker of uneasiness, but found only indignation, coupled with honest, straightforward impatience. And slowly, his anger melted away. "Maybe you just *think* you saw the murder…or you were influenced by Gray and the sheriff."

She threw her hands in the air. "Whatever."

"Think about it. If my dad didn't kill Wes Truly, then who did? And if this guy is still around, is he worried now you and I are both back in town? You're the last major witness, and I'm sure word has spread about me asking people questions about that night."

She swallowed hard. "I suppose—if the murderer is someone else—that he'd want both of us to leave…."

He rested one booted foot on the porch rail. "Do you or Michael have any idea who might have broken into the clinic?"

"He's investigating it right now, but I'm guessing that he won't find a single significant fingerprint."

"No witnesses, then?"

She shook her head. "Someone seems determined to cause trouble, and is smart enough to cover his tracks. And," she added on a long sigh, "he's definitely escalating. The question is—how long can I hold on, before he ruins my business or someone gets hurt?"

*   *   *

The move to the Brownley place had seemed
perfectly logical to Leigh. To Claire, it approxi-
mated an act of treason.

"How could you even think of moving there?"
she snapped the moment Leigh walked in the door
at Snow Canyon Lodge. She propped her hands on
her bony hips, stalked to the windows overlooking the mountains, then folded her arms across
her chest and whirled around. "And don't think I
didn't hear about it, young lady. If not for that
man, Gray never would have sold out. Not like he
did, sneaky and underhanded, without a word to
me. And ask yourself—if that deal was fair,
where's all the money?"

Leigh opened her mouth, then shut it, unable to
fire back a logical response.

It was true. Gray had always talked about leaving
the ranch to Leigh and her sisters, and probably
Claire as well. If he'd needed the money, why hadn't
he at least offered to sell it to them? He hadn't told
anyone, even though he and Leigh had talked on the
phone at least once a month the year before he'd
died. Then again, given their lifelong bickering and
the undercurrent of competition between Gray and
Claire, maybe he'd considered this the moment to
have the final word.

But the money—that was another issue.

Cole was a handsome, charming man with undeniable charisma. Even as a teenager, he'd drawn the attention of all the girls in town with his dark, brooding good looks. Now, he was successful. Accomplished. And a loving father. Had she fallen under his spell, only to forget the true circumstances of his presence in Wolf Creek?

Claire's eyes narrowed. "See? Something was really wrong about that deal. And you running off to set up house on that man's property is wrong, too."

"It's only temporary, and it was the best option I could find in a hurry. And I'm not staying in his house, if that's what you think." Leigh fingered the keys in her pocket. "So, are you set to go? You have an appointment at four o'clock."

It was Claire's turn to fall silent.

"With your doctor." Leigh started for the door, hoping her mother would follow, but she stubbornly held her ground. "We'll be late, Claire."

"I...think I'll just stay here."

"Janna told me this appointment has been set up for months. The doctor only comes to Wolf Creek once a week, and it's been a long time since you've been seen." She turned back and gently looped her arm around Claire's elbow. "Please?"

"Why do you care? Why do any of you care? Just let me be."

"Because we l—" Leigh stumbled over the word, one that was so foreign in her relationships with her mother and sisters. The emotion was buried so deep, beneath layers of hurt and anger, that the word lodged in her throat.

"Because we love you," she said firmly. "Because we care about you, and want you to stay healthy and strong and happy."

Claire's eyes blazed with sudden anger as she looked around the bedroom that she had made her own prison because she so rarely agreed to leave it. A silent rebellion that her mother was still waging over the fact that she no longer could live independently in her own home.

Claire's shoulders sagged in defeat. "Let's go then," she muttered. "I really don't care."

Deafening silence filled the truck as Leigh drove to town, despite one attempt after another to draw her mother into a conversation.

She drummed her fingertips on the steering wheel. "Doc Adams called me back this morning. The insurance adjuster is coming from Jackson today to look over the clinic."

Silence.

"I guess Adams kept an adequate policy on the place, so unless the adjuster says it's a total loss, I'll soon be able to schedule an appointment with the contractor."

Claire snorted. "That building shoulda been knocked down years ago. Adams never sunk a penny in that place. It's a firetrap."

"Then I suppose there's a chance that he'll have

to rebuild, which wouldn't be a bad thing. Right? Either way, the building will probably be better than it ever was before, and I'll still have the same contract on it."

Claire just harrumphed and looked out her window.

At the north edge of town, Leigh slowed down and turned on her left-hand signal, then steered into the doctor's parking lot and pulled to a stop.

She turned to look at Claire. "All set?"

Her mother sat silent and still, making no move to get out of the truck.

"Is there something wrong?" Leigh felt a flash of alarm. "Are you okay?"

Strong and domineering all her life, Claire had prided herself on never showing weakness, and she'd demanded the same of her daughters, even when they were young.

But now, her fingers were trembling ever so slightly and Leigh could see the rapid rise and fall of her chest. "What's wrong? Should I run in and get help?"

"No." Claire lifted her chin in typical McAllister fashion, grabbed the door handle and got out of the truck. She marched up the sidewalk to the door of the office with the air of someone going off to war.

Mystified, Leigh followed her.

When they got back to Snow Canyon Lodge, Leigh

and Janna needed to talk. Because something was wrong, and Claire probably wouldn't ever admit it.

Inside the clinic, Leigh sat in a chair right next to Claire's and took one of her gnarled hands in both of hers.

And for the first time Leigh could remember, Claire didn't pull away.

Claire chose to go in to see the doctor alone.

When she came out, she strode through the waiting room and went out the front door without a word to Leigh.

Leigh looked up at the nurse who was still standing in the doorway leading back to the exam rooms, a stack of charts cradled in her arm. "Can I talk to you for a second?" Leigh asked.

The nurse glanced at the elderly couple seated across the room. "You have an appointment?"

"I just brought my mother in—Mrs. McAllister. Is there any chance that I could speak to the doctor about her?"

A flicker of humor showed in the woman's eyes. "Mrs. McAllister has been quite adamant about not signing the privacy forms that would allow family members access to her medical information." The nurse glanced down the hall behind her, then edged closer to Leigh and lowered her voice. "Honestly, I think it would be a good idea. We see a lot of folks who are getting on in years, and allowing their families to help with medical decisions would be to their benefit."

It was Leigh's turn to look behind her, to make sure no one would overhear. "Is there anything we can do? To…um…get that permission anyhow?"

The nurse shook her head. "Only by a court order from a judge, ruling your mother incompetent. I'm sorry—but you can't imagine the legal trouble I could be in if I provided personal information to you. And the doctor is in the same position."

"I understand. Thanks." Leigh turned to go, but the woman touched her hand.

"This might be a good time to really talk to your mother, and try to reason with her about this," she whispered. "I've been down this road myself, and I know it isn't an easy one."

On the way home, Leigh tried to make casual conversation about cattle prices. The drought. Local political issues. Claire answered in monosyllables, if at all, clearly disinterested and distracted by something she refused to talk about.

When Leigh pulled to a stop in front of the lodge, she said a silent prayer and turned to her mother once more. "I know something is bothering you. I really want to help—we all do. But if you don't say anything, we can't make things easier for you. Now, I know you were upset on the way to the doctor's office. They can't say anything to me without your permission, so I'm asking you—is something wrong?"

"I do not get 'upset,'" she said in a curt tone as she opened her door. "And there's nothing to concern yourself about."

With a heavy heart, Leigh stood outside her truck watching her mother march up to the lodge and go inside. At a soft chuckle, she turned and found Janna walking up the lane with an armload of fresh towels.

"Even if I hadn't known that you were taking Claire to the doctor, I'd know from your expression that you'd just spent time with her. She can be challenging, can't she?"

"And frustrating, and worrisome. Tell me, do you know what this appointment was for?"

"A six-month checkup on her blood pressure."

"Does she let you go back into the exam room with her? Does she let you talk to the doctors?"

"Are you kidding?" Janna shook her head slowly, her resignation clear. "Not even Tessa is privy to that. When she started showing signs of confusion, the local doctors sent her to a neurologist. He insisted on being able to talk to the family, and she finally agreed to that. We'll eventually need to have power of attorney forms drawn up, but she's not at all willing to discuss the future."

Leigh sighed. "Well, I can tell you that she was really nervous about something while we were driving into town. And she wasn't any happier on the drive home."

That earned a short laugh. "I'm afraid *happy* and *Claire* aren't words that go together very often. I'll try to talk to her and find out what's going on." Janna smiled, then gave Leigh a quick, one-armed hug. "You know the one good thing about all of this? After all these years, we're finally talking. I missed you and Tessa so much after I left home."

Leigh closed her eyes briefly as painful memories surfaced. "I don't think I forgave you for years, for moving out," Leigh finally admitted. "I kept waiting and waiting, hoping you would come back for me, and you never did."

"I was in college. I had no money." Janna's eyes shimmered. "But Mother was better once I left, wasn't she? That's what I always hoped."

It hadn't been better, but Leigh just nodded. "I only hope one of us can get through to that stony heart of hers before it's too late."

ELEVEN

Cole reined his bay gelding next to Leigh's paint mare. "I haven't seen Brianna this happy since the last time we all went riding."

They'd gone several times now, following rugged trails high up into the mountains. Picnicking by crystalline mountain streams.

"What little girl wouldn't love having a pretty horse to ride?" Leigh smiled. "I'll bet she sleeps well tonight, after all these hours on the trail. You might have trouble getting her up tomorrow."

"You're probably right." He pulled to a halt in the shade of a tall stand of pines. "But I've been out of town far too many weekends, and I look forward to finally going to church with Polly and her. You're welcome to come along, if you'd like. No sense in all of us driving that far."

Maybe so, but arriving in his company would probably set off gossip about a personal relationship that didn't exist. *Not yet, anyway,* a small voice whispered, maybe someday...

Of course, that sort of thinking was just crazy.

Brianna had been coming over to the vet clinic every afternoon this week, enthralled with the animals and the idea of becoming a vet just like Leigh, and Cole had been stopping by to pick her up. Though the cool reserve between Leigh and him had started to thaw, there was no sense in imagining any deeper relationship in the future. Yesterday, Brianna had shown Leigh some photographs of all the pets she'd had when she was younger.

Cole and his ex-wife were in some of the photos, and Alicia was beautiful. Not just beautiful—but a true show-stopper who could have swept all the beauty pageants with her exotic looks and stunning figure.

A man couldn't possibly go from Miss America to a five-foot-two country vet in coveralls and muddy boots.

Ahead, Brianna nudged her palomino into a slow, easy jog. "Watching her sure brings back memories," Leigh said.

"I imagine you and your sisters were mostly working when you were on horseback, though." Cole leaned forward and brushed a fly off his gelding's neck, then settled back in his saddle. "So that couldn't have been much fun."

"Actually it was." Leigh breathed in the fresh

scents of pine and sagebrush, and tilted her face up to receive the warmth of the afternoon sun. "Especially when we moved cattle up into the summer ranges or brought them back down in the fall. We pretended we were in a John Wayne movie, most of the time."

Cole laughed. "I used to imagine I was in those old cowboy movies as a kid, too." He shook out some extra slack in his reins. "You've probably noticed that Brianna thinks *you're* quite a star. She talks about you and your clinic nonstop." His voice grew serious. "But honestly, you don't have to feel obligated. If she's any trouble at all, send her home. The housekeeper could be there in five minutes flat."

"She's been no problem, and if I need to leave on ranch calls, I just drop her off at your house. She's an awesome kid, by the way. Smart as can be, and with the greatest questions." Leigh slid a sideways look at him. "But you'd better be prepared. She's been naming those orphaned puppies, and if she has her way, she'll be adopting every last one of them."

"I know. She talks about them—in the most melodramatic terms. It's been really hard on her to be away from her mother so much, and I think she's transferring some of her feelings onto them."

The trail led into a cool stand of pines where they had to ride single file, then out into a meadow rimmed with quaking aspen.

"Thanks again for letting me use those buildings," Leigh said when he urged his horse forward to catch up with hers. "I know there's a lot of old baggage between us, and I would've understood if you'd said no."

He shrugged. "Your uncle wanted you to use them in the first place, and it's no trouble. Have you heard from your contractor?"

"Doc Adams's insurance is covering all of the water damage, but I can't get anyone to start working on the place for at least three weeks. And then, it's going to take time to get it all done. You've really been a lifesaver."

"As I said, you can stay as long as you like. It isn't any problem."

"The irony is that you've been gracious, but my mother is still angry about Gray selling this place. She'll barely speak to me now that I've moved over here." Leigh reached for the water bottle hanging from her saddle horn and took a long swallow, then angled a glance at Cole from under the brim of her hat. "I thought you should know, in case you ever run into her. She's sure Gray's sale came about through nefarious doings on your part, and that you really took him to the cleaners on the deal."

He laughed. "My accountant wouldn't agree. This place was a shade under market value, but I had to sell off most of my investment properties in California to swing it. And your uncle certainly could've refused my offer."

From everything she'd seen of Cole since moving here, she knew he spoke the truth. Yet...

"The one thing I don't understand is that he never said anything to the family about selling out. I grew up knowing that someday, my sisters and I would inherit Four Winds, because that's what he'd always wanted—to keep his land in the family."

She waited, hoping Cole might volunteer something about Gray's frame of mind over the sale, but he didn't. "Did he ever say anything to you about why he was selling?"

"My Realtor told me about several properties available in the area, so I flew back and took a look. But I never saw Gray when I was given a tour, and my lawyer handled the sale. All I did was sign the papers." Cole's voice grew sympathetic. "I'm sorry."

"I...didn't mean to imply that I was blaming you in any way. Your business was with him, not the rest of us."

They rode on into the shadows of the mountains, through a deep stream where they let the horses drink, and then down the long stretch leading to the corrals and barns of the ranch.

Brianna was already unsaddling her horse by the time Cole and Leigh pulled to a stop at the hitching rail. She ducked under her horse's neck, her eyes shining and with a smile that lit up her whole face.

As soon as Cole dismounted, she rushed up to him and wrapped her arms around his waist. "This was the best present ever," she exclaimed. "Glitter is the prettiest horse in the world. I can't wait to send Mom some pictures!"

"She's a very lucky girl," Leigh said, watching Brianna lead her horse to the pasture gate.

"I think we both know that those old-timers she rescued will never be sound enough for much riding. I wanted her to have fun here, and not miss home quite so much."

Leigh started unsaddling her own horse. "You don't think she'll ever go back to live with her mom?"

"Alicia's new fiancé is much older, and wealthy enough to give her everything she could possibly want. But he wants a pretty trophy wife, not more children to raise." Cole snorted in disgust. "It will hurt Brianna badly if she ever realizes how easily she was traded off. I'm the lucky one in this deal, because now I have custody."

A warm feeling spread through Leigh as she watched him finish taking the saddle off his horse.

"Leigh?"

She suddenly realized he was watching her, a smile tipping up a corner of his mouth. "Sorry—daydreaming, I guess."

"If you're still game, I think Polly is planning on

you staying for supper. Brianna really hopes you'll stay, too."

And what about you?

But of course, that was a foolish thought.

He was simply her landlord, nothing more. He was also recovering from a difficult divorce, while she had no time for anything approaching a romance—especially with someone who had dumped her once before. She wouldn't let that happen again.

And while a few trail rides could be construed as casual fellowship, a dinner in Cole's house—*Gray's* old house—was a step she didn't want to take.

"I—I appreciate the invitation, but I can't."

Brianna came bounding back from the pasture. "Please, *stay!*"

I...um...really don't think—"

The child's face crumpled. "But Polly made a special dessert, just 'cause you were coming. And I could show you my room, and my Breyer model horses, and everything. Please? We never have company."

"She doesn't have time, sweetheart." Cole's voice cooled, his expression turned distant. "She's a very busy lady."

It was the perfect moment to walk away. He'd just given her an easy exit.

But at the heartfelt disappointment in Brianna's eyes, Leigh just couldn't refuse.

* * *

Cole had intended to pave the way for some careful questioning by taking Leigh trail riding and plying her with dinner and friendly conversation.

He hadn't planned on noticing the delicate scent of her perfume, or the way her long, strawberry-blond hair seemed to capture sunlight and gleam with a light all its own. And he hadn't planned on a simple supper of grilled steaks and twice-baked potatoes lasting for nearly two hours while he got caught up in her laughter and intelligent conversation. He'd misjudged her all these years, hanging on to his negative misperceptions, when he should have been listening to his heart.

And now he'd discovered, to his chagrin, that the woman who had symbolized everything that had gone wrong in his life could now mesmerize him with a single, sidelong glance.

"I'll walk you out to your truck," he said after Brianna excused herself and went upstairs. "But I'm also going to follow you home. I don't want you going back to that place in the dark."

Leigh smiled as they strolled side by side out to the driveway. "I'm a big girl. I can handle it."

"Not on my watch. And speaking of that, call me if you ever have to go out on ranch calls during the night. I'd be glad to go along, or meet you when you get home. Or I can send a ranch hand."

"Ranch hand? You found somebody?"

"Lowell never showed up. But I did hire a couple of guys named Bob and Denny, who worked on the Rocking M. The owner is selling out, so it was good timing for me, and they come with good recommendations." Cole opened the door of her truck for her, then rolled the tension out of his shoulders. "And none too soon. Keeping up with this place is way too much for one person, and I've got some training horses coming in the first of the month."

She buckled her seat belt and turned on the ignition. "Sounds like you'll still be busy. Thanks again for supper and a wonderful afternoon."

He watched her drive down the lane as he got in his own truck and started the engine. Maybe she thought he shouldn't bother, but the idea of her staying alone still made him uneasy. Anyone could be lurking in the darkness.

Behind the barn.

At the corner of the cabin.

Or even be waiting inside.

And until the sheriff figured out who was after her, Cole would do his best to keep her safe.

Cole went into the barn with Leigh while she checked on the animals, then walked around the exterior of the building.

He took the same care when she went to the cabin, first checking outside and then looking into every room.

"Satisfied?" she said with a smile. "I told you everything would be okay. Remember—I've got my trusty guard dog here to protect me."

"He's quite a fireball," Cole admitted with a laugh. "I'm sure he could scare the dickens out of anyone who dared try to break in."

Hobo, comfortably curled up on a rug by the refrigerator had barely lifted his head when they'd walked in the door, but then he seemed to be a dog that valued an economy of movement. "Since you came all this way, could I offer you some tea?"

Cole hesitated. "Maybe out on your porch?"

She gathered a tray with glasses of tea and a plate of Oreos and took them out to the small wrought-iron-and-glass ice-cream table that she'd set up this morning.

Cole studied her somberly. "I don't mean to dredge up a lot of bad memories for you. But I'd like to ask you a few questions about the trial. Do you mind?"

Disappointment lanced through her. *So that's why he was being so nice.* It wasn't because he cared about her—he just wanted access to information. She should have known.

"I imagine you've requested all of the old court reports by now. There's nothing else I can tell you—when I was on the stand I told them exactly what I saw, and during the cross-examination I answered every question they had about that night."

He reached across the table and rested a hand on

top of one of hers. Meant to be a gentle, comforting touch, probably, but it sent a spark of sensation zinging up her arm and she reflexively drew her hand back.

"Sorry," he said with a rueful smile. "But this means a lot to me. Now that Gray is gone, you're the only real witness left."

"And I didn't see the actual murder." She heaved a sigh. "Look, I'll do my best. But you've got to understand that this happened almost seventeen years ago. My memory isn't perfect. And if I recall something differently now, you'd be better off believing those court transcripts, anyway."

"Understood."

She closed her eyes, remembering that dark night outside the Hilltop Tavern. Trying to sort imagination and later nightmares from fact.

"I was fifteen. I'd been with my uncle that day, at a cattle auction, and Gray was taking me home. We drove through town, but when he saw a certain truck parked at the tavern, he stopped and backed up. He told me to stay inside his pickup with the windows up halfway and the doors locked. There was some rancher inside, and Gray wanted to hand him a check. So he found a spot to park maybe thirty feet from the building, and said he'd be back in just a couple minutes."

"So Gray went inside."

"That's right. But he was gone a lot longer than

a couple minutes. There was some sort of scuffle going on inside over a poker game. I don't remember all of the names, but they did come up at the trial."

"Ed Quinton. Wes Truly. Don Miller. Gabe Brown. My father. There were at least four other guys who'd dropped out because the stakes had skyrocketed. None of the witnesses ever agreed on who they all were, but it was a smoky, crowded, hole-in-the-wall place, and a lot of the guys were pretty well drunk by then."

"See? You know more than me, anyway."

"But I wasn't *there*." He casually rubbed at the condensation of his glass as if perfectly relaxed, but he held her gaze with laser-sharp intensity. "So what happened after your uncle went inside?"

"I fidgeted, probably, wishing he would hurry. It was dark, and the security light didn't reach where we'd parked."

"What did it cover?"

She frowned, picturing the scene in her head. "It was on a tall telephone pole set at the front, south-west corner of the building. So it covered the front and south sides quite well. Less toward the back, of course."

"And you had an unobstructed view?"

"There were other trucks and cars, but a few had left, so I could see the building well. Not that I was really looking…until I heard something." She shivered, remembering that awful, guttural moan. And then a harsh curse in a deeper voice.

"Go on."

"I leaned forward and looked out. I saw a long shape on the ground. It took a second to register, because I just couldn't believe it—but then I could make out the guy's boots, with the toes pointing up. Suddenly everything seemed sharper. More clear. Like adrenaline was rushing through me. You know, the old fight-or-flight response."

"He was alone?"

"I wish, but you know the answer to that. Your dad was there, standing over the body. He had a knife in his left hand—held down at his side. The top part near the hilt glittered in the light. The bottom part was dark. Dark and wet. I wanted to scream, but I didn't dare. I was afraid he would come after me because I'd seen him. And then a lot of people came out of the front doors of the tavern, and your dad tried to run. I didn't see it happen, but during the trial someone said he took the knife with him and threw it in the bushes."

"You're sure it was my dad."

"I'd seen him at dozens of rodeos, Cole. Up close, because sometimes he and Gray would talk. I recognized his hat with the brim bent down, his bright yellow shirt, and his square jaw. That loose-limbed way he walked. And when he swore, I recognized his voice."

"Did you see him knock Wes Truly down and drive the knife into the center of the man's chest?"

Leigh's stomach rolled. "No."

"If there'd been a fight outside you would have heard and seen it, because you were close enough to see the gleam of the knife."

"Right. But I didn't notice anything, until suddenly there they were—your dad, and that man on the ground. Maybe they came out through the back door of the tavern."

"But there wasn't a struggle. And the guy wasn't dead yet, or you wouldn't have heard him groan."

"Right."

Cole stood and paced to the end of the porch, then returned, rubbing the back of his neck. "Gray testified that he walked in on a fight inside the tavern. There were men throwing punches and shoving each other, and a few were on the floor. Gray said he saw my father arguing with Wes. Threatening him, because apparently the guy was a cheat and cleaned almost everyone out of everything they had. Some of the players were pretty desperate about the money they'd lost."

Leigh nodded. "That sounds about right."

"Is there anything else you can remember? Anything at all?"

An image flitted at the edges of her memory. A frightening, ethereal image that disappeared as quickly as it had come. "There was chaos, just minutes later. People yelling. Rushing around. Some of them ran out to the parking lot and left. But one guy in a western hat and a long oilskin coat ran past Gray's truck and saw me inside. He warned me to keep my mouth shut about things I didn't know. But I never saw his face. The sheriff figured it might've been one of Rand's buddies—or someone in a panic that night. I'm sorry. There's nothing else I can say."

"Did the sheriff follow up on that guy? Ask you any more questions?"

She nodded. "He questioned me a couple times. I kept asking about the guy in the coat, and the sheriff said he found him—then grilled him at length. It was just some ranch hand."

"Did he testify?"

"I don't remember. I wasn't there for every day of the trial. And anyway, I was just a kid, Cole. I wouldn't have thought to question anyone about what the lawyers did."

He studied her for a long moment. "If you think of anything—anything at all—come and tell me, okay?"

She nodded, picking up on his frustration and wishing she could be of more help. "I don't understand. Your father's gone, bless his soul, and he took the blame. So if someone else killed Wes, he ought to feel safe."

"I went to visit Gabe Brown last Friday. He didn't remember me, but he sure remembered my last name. I told him I wanted to ask questions about the night of the murder, and he seemed frightened. He made me close the door before he would talk, but then he barely said anything before ordering me out of his room. Not six hours later he was dead."

"Dead?" She shivered at a sudden chill. "But he was probably old, right? With health problems?"

"That's what the care center and his doctor figured. Most of the old folks never have an autopsy in that kind of situation. I called his doctor though, and talked to her at length. She isn't convinced, but she did finally agree to order an autopsy. The results won't be in for a couple weeks, though."

"What about the sheriff?"

"After I talked to Dr. Lohman, I called Michael and relayed my concerns. It's a hazy situation, given Gabe's poor health. I understand the man was suffering from end-stage lung cancer, and he could've gone at any time. I'm just not convinced that his cancer got him. I think somebody hurried him along to our Maker because they were afraid he would say too much." Cole moved to stand next to her. "That's why I want you to be careful. If someone murdered Gabe, he might not stop there."

Cole settled a hand on her shoulder in a comforting gesture, but there was far more than just simple reassurance, now. It was as if he'd finally accepted that she'd told the truth about the murder scene, exactly as she'd seen it play out. The depth of caring and concern was something new, and it sent warmth curling around her heart.

Drawn by the emotion in his eyes, she fought a sudden temptation to step closer to him.

"Promise you'll call me if you have late-night vet calls, or feel the slightest bit uneasy about anything. Okay?"

She nodded.

"In the meantime, I'm trying to talk to everyone I can find who was at the tavern the night Wes died. So far, Don Miller refused to talk to me, then suddenly left town on the pretext of visiting relatives. Ed Quinton was gone every time I stopped at his place."

"So now what?"

"I'm going back to Ed's tomorrow, first thing after church. I have a hunch that some of the others in town are going to be afraid to talk, like Gabe was. But *someone* has to remember the names of the other guys who were present that night. And if I can find them, I should be very close to uncovering the truth."

He smiled and cupped her face between his large, warm hands, sending another shiver through her, and brushed a kiss against her forehead.

"And then, Dr. McAllister, I'd like to spend some time with you. Because we need to talk."

TWELVE

Cole called on Sunday morning to offer Leigh a ride to church. Brianna got on the phone and begged.

But Leigh knew small-town gossips too well to take that chance.

"I'll see you there," she said with a laugh. "Believe me—it's better that way. And if I happen to get an emergency call on my cell phone, it'll just save time to have my truck there. But thanks anyway."

Now, walking up the long sidewalk to the entrance of the church, she tipped her head back and looked at the tall, beautiful spire, with its lacy, gingerbread trim, and felt a familiar sense of peace and belonging.

Old friends and neighbors nodded to her, their smiles warm and welcoming. And up by the massive oak doors, Pastor Lindsberg stood in his white robes—a massive bear of a man with the gentlest smile and best sense of humor she'd ever encountered.

He reached out to grasp her hand for a vigorous shake, one hand at her elbow. "We've missed you," he boomed, his eyes twinkling. "Sure glad to have you back."

"I'll be better, promise." She smiled back at him. "Last Sunday I had an emergency farm call, the weekend before that I had to do surgery on a dog that someone abandoned on my doorstep."

He nodded sagely. "All God's creatures, every one of them. Jesus healed on the Sabbath, too, so I'm sure He understands. The ranchers are lucky to have a good veterinarian in these parts."

Not all of them seemed to think so. Business was still far less than she'd expected, but she just smiled. "Thanks."

He nodded toward the open doors. "Some of your family is already inside. I'm still hoping to see your mother and Tessa one of these days, though."

She met his gaze and saw only understanding and compassion in his faded blue eyes. "I'd like that, too. Believe me."

Inside the cool depths of the church, she felt a deep sense of comfort wash through her as she breathed in the scents of the candles flickering softly at the front of the church and listened to the white-haired organist—Mrs. Sawyer, still at it after all these years—playing a soft rendition of "Beautiful Savior."

Sunlight sparkled through the intricate jewel-toned stained-glass windows flanking each side of the church, casting colorful patterns across the oak pews. The altar was simple, leading the eye to the beautiful stained-glass window that soared above it.

As a child, she'd been entranced by the rendition of Jesus and his flock, but now it never failed to touch her on a deeper, more spiritual level.

At a rustle of movement, she scanned the hundred or so parishioners who were already seated and found Janna, Rylie, Michael and Ian halfway up on the left. Rylie grinned and wiggled her fingers, motioning Leigh to join them.

To the right near the back, Cole and Brianna sat with their housekeeper—and Brianna was eagerly extending the same invitation.

Torn, Leigh hesitated, then slid into the pew next to Brianna, who probably knew far fewer people here than Rylie did.

Leigh leaned close and pointed surreptitiously toward Rylie. "Have you met my niece?" she whispered. "She's just a couple of years younger than you."

Brianna nodded and grinned. "We're in the same class in Sunday school!"

Leigh settled back in her pew, thankful that the old system of combining several grade levels was still in place. In such a small congregation, it meant the kids got to know each other better, and it fostered friendships between the rural and town kids who were otherwise spread great distances apart.

She glanced over Brianna's head and caught Cole looking at her with an unreadable expression in his dark eyes, but then the congregation stood to begin singing the first hymn of the day.

Was he disappointed in her answers last night? Did he think she'd held back information, and that she'd just recited what everyone knew about the night of the murder?

She'd tried. *Honestly* tried to remember everything that had happened that night, though long after Cole had left, she'd still felt that old jittery, unsettled feeling in her stomach, and when she'd finally fallen asleep—well after two in the morning—her old nightmare had returned. The same as always.

And as always, the dream had left her sweating and shaking, her heart pounding against her ribs. Even as an adult, the images were as powerful and terrifying as ever.

Now, she felt Cole's large, warm hand enclose one of hers and squeeze gently. Drawing in a faltering breath, she looked up and found him watching her with an expression of concern.

"You look pale," he murmured. "Are you all right? Do you need to step outside for a while?"

Embarrassed, she felt heat rise in her cheeks as she shook her head and turned back to the pulpit, where Pastor Lindsberg was reciting the Gospel verse of the day.

"'There is no fear in love, but perfect love casts out fear. For fear has to do with punishment, and he who fears is not perfected in love.' I John 4:18." He turned to another page in his Bible. "And our second verse is found in Matthew, chapter six, verse twenty-four. 'Therefore do not be anxious about tomorrow, for tomorrow will be anxious for itself.'"

The pastor looked out over the congregation and braced his palms on the pulpit. "There's an old English proverb that states, 'Fear knocked at the door and Faith answered. There was no one there.' So I ask you—what is the better choice? Despair in the face of fear, or the full confidence and joy of accepting our Creator's power and love, which passes all understanding?"

Leigh shifted in her seat. *Fear.* Despite maturity and adult logic, it had lodged in the dark recesses of her memory ever since that terrible night, wrapped in vague, threatening images that she couldn't quite identify.

But as it so often happened, the verses and sermon seemed meant just for her. It was time to let go, and let God take over. Had she ever really asked Him for that?

She bowed her head as the pastor began his sermon. *Please Lord, I'm so tired. I've let the past haunt me all these years when I should have just given all of my fears over to You. Please, take this burden away. If there's any hidden meaning to it, help me to*

*see the truth—and then help me leave it behind and
walk in Your light. In Jesus's name, I pray.*

Leigh had been only half-serious when she'd
given Cole the excuse that taking her own truck to
church would be more convenient, in case she
received any emergency calls. But sure enough,
there was one waiting on the voice mail of her
silenced cell phone when the service ended.

Quickly giving her apologies to Janna—who'd
extended a standing invitation to Sunday dinner the
first day Leigh had moved back to town—she darted
out the side door of the church to avoid the delay of
friendly conversations with the congregation.

At her truck, she pulled a pair of coveralls over
her slacks and sweater, donned a pair of western
boots and climbed behind the wheel.

Cole appeared at her door before she could start
the engine. "Is everything all right?"

"I have an emergency call." She turned the key
in the ignition. "Did you need something?"

He frowned. "Since you work alone and don't
have a receptionist yet, you should always tell
someone where you're going. At least until Michael
finds the guy who's been harassing you."

"I'm not sure who I would tell, Cole. Everyone's
busy with their own lives as it is." She glanced at
her watch. "Look, I'm on my way to the Wilkinson
ranch, and I really need to leave."

"I heard that Max is working there now."

That gave her a moment's pause. "Well, if he's there, I'll just be pleasant and nonchalant. I can certainly take care of myself."

Cole backed away from her door, his eyes somber. "Just watch your back, okay?"

Watch your back—in sleepy little Wolf Creek, where the biggest crime during any given week might be someone driving five miles over the speed limit?

The irony wasn't amusing, and the truth of it sent a chill through her…because he was right. "Thanks, Cole."

But he'd already turned away, and over the noise of the truck he probably didn't hear her.

"Good job," she muttered to herself. *Be rude to a man who was only trying to be kind.* But there was no time to go after him, and she would have to apologize later.

At the Wilkinson ranch, she found Ray Wilkinson waiting impatiently in front of his barn. He scowled as she got out of the truck with her emergency bag.

"Took you an hour to get here," he growled. "If there'd been another clinic in the area, I would've called them instead."

"I'm sorry. I had my cell phone turned off during church, but got here quick as I could. What's up?"

"Laceration—long and deep. I have no idea what

happened—we had this bull on five acres of good pasture. Strong fence, absolutely no junk out there. The boys managed to run him into a stock trailer to bring him home."

The man led her through a long horse barn, past several corrals and into another barn. Everything on the place was neat, well kept and spoke of money.

The bull was lying down in a small corral, his head up, and he blew noisily out his nostrils at the approach of visitors. A deep laceration stretched across his mud-caked side, exposing cherry-red muscle and glimpses of pale white ribs.

"You don't know how this happened?"

"Not a clue. My boys searched the pasture and couldn't find anything unusual."

"Has he been handled much?"

The man snorted. "Are you asking if you can just go in there and treat him while he lays there?"

She bit back a retort. "Of course not. I'm wondering if you have a treatment chute anywhere close by, so we can confine him long enough to clean up that wound and suture it…and I'm wondering if it's going to be a big fight getting him there."

Ray turned on his heel. "Boys?"

Two ranch hands appeared from a feed room. The first was a lanky young kid she'd never seen before. The second was Max, whose expression hardened as soon as he saw her.

"Run him into the chute," Ray barked. "And

watch out for that wound. I can't afford to let him get any worse."

Max and the other hand opened a series of gates and drove the bull through each narrow passage, leading the animal closer to his destination.

At last, he was funneled into a brightly lit state-of-the-art barn where he was faced with a dead end and a gate slammed shut behind him. The bull snorted. Pawed. Slammed his great weight side-ways, until the men were finally able to secure his massive neck in a hydraulic head gate—curved, vertical bars that firmly held him in place.

"Right now, he's an unhappy, three-quarter ton moving target," Leigh muttered as she prepared a syringe of lidocaine. "But he'll settle down in a few minutes. And once I numb the wound, he won't feel a thing. Do you have warm water out here? Clean buckets?"

Ray flicked a glance at Max, and the man trotted over to the wall, where there were spigots, neatly coiled hoses and upended buckets. "So tell me—what do you think of this animal?"

She knew he was testing her, but she hadn't grown up on a ranch and finished four years of vet school for nothing. "Nice. Good top line, beautiful balance. Excellent muscling. One of the best Angus bulls I've seen."

Ray looked satisfied, and Leigh figured she passed.

Max returned with two stainless-steel buckets

and a hose with a spray-nozzle attachment. He leveled a long, eerie look at Leigh before turning toward Ray. "I've got it running lukewarm, boss."

"Good. Now, let's sit back and watch this little lady work."

"Little lady," Leigh grumbled to herself as she did the last of her chores at the clinic that evening. In some contexts, it might be meant as a sweet, loving address.

Ray Wilkinson had meant it as anything but. He'd watched her every move as she'd thoroughly cleaned the wound of debris, excised the ragged edges, then had carefully closed each layer with perfect, even sutures.

After a tetanus booster and a first dose of antibiotics, the bull had been turned back into a spacious, deeply bedded stall, where he'd attacked his feed with vigor.

So when the phone rang early the next morning, Leigh wasn't prepared for the sound of Ray Wilkinson's furious voice.

"I don't know what you did out here, but that bull is *dead*."

Stunned, she stared at the phone for a second before placing it back at her ear. "I checked his heart rate, respirations and temperature before he left the stocks. He moved just fine back to his stall. He was on his feet and eating when I left."

"No dice, Doc. You obviously gave him the

wrong drug—something that didn't hit him until later. I just hope you have real good malpractice insurance, because I'm going to recover every last penny."

THIRTEEN

Ray Wilkinson might have seemed like a short-spoken man, but he clearly knew how to spread word around a community.

By noon—mere hours after his phone call about the bull—no less than eight of her upcoming appointments to do herd work at local ranches had been canceled.

"I know it wasn't my error," she said to Cole the minute he walked in the door of her temporary clinic. Brianna tagged along behind him and made a beeline for the puppy cage in back.

"That bull had strong vital signs before and after I started. He was fairly quiet in the chute—settled right down once the boys closed the head gate. I didn't need to risk using a sedative, and I used lidocaine so he wouldn't be in any pain while I sutured him. He didn't suffer anything even remotely close to stress of general surgery." She drew a deep breath. "And I did a blood draw before I left. His blood values indicated absolutely no sign of internal bleeding from his accident." She paused. "Max was there, though. And he seemed, I don't…"

Cole leaned on the door frame, looking thoughtful.

Leigh continued. "He didn't say a word, and I didn't either. I was busy, and he kept his distance. If he was afraid I'd say something to his boss about what happened at your place, he was wrong."

"He could have done something to the bull to retaliate."

"With any number of drugs, I suppose. But I just can't imagine he'd do such a thing. Ray told me the bull was worth a tremendous amount of money and would be extremely hard to replace. Why would Max jeopardize his new job just to get back at me?"

"You never know. What about infection at the wound site?"

"I started that bull on a broad-spectrum, high-powered antibiotic, and I gave him a loading dose—a high initial dose to kick it off more quickly."

"In other words, there's no plausible medical reason for that bull to die related to the services you provided."

"Exactly. Which is why I want to go back to that ranch and draw samples for a postmortem toxicology report. A necropsy would be even better, in case something else happened by coincidence.

Some sort of heart failure, or brain damage…but the chances of that seem nearly impossible."

"Maybe Max shot him. Somewhere where a bullet wound wouldn't easily show."

"A necropsy would uncover that as well. But when I asked Ray, he refused—even though I offered it at no charge. He said, 'You've done enough,' and that he didn't want me back on his property. But in the meantime, this could completely ruin my reputation."

"Do you want me to run out there with you?"

"To see if you can make him cooperate?"

"Something like that. Seems to me that he's being totally unreasonable."

"I'll be fine. Surely the man would like some answers, if he stops to think about it. And free— what's not to like?"

Cole frowned. "I'd feel better if I could go along. Ray concerns me, and I just don't trust Max."

"You certainly don't need to—" She stopped short, suddenly recognizing the gift Cole was offering. Support. Concern for her safety. Just as he had when she'd rushed off on that ill-fated vet call.

Independence and hard work had been drilled into her from early childhood. Asking for help had often earned a caustic remark from her mother or taunts from her older sisters, who'd thought she was just an irritating tagalong. But was it so wrong to accept his gracious offer?

"Thanks, Cole," she amended. "I…I'm sorry I've been so blunt lately. Can Brianna stay with your housekeeper? I'm not sure this visit would be appropriate for her."

"Absolutely. That was my thought exactly."

The drive to the Wilkinson ranch seemed much shorter with Cole for company. On the way, they shared old high-school rodeo stories, and despite her tension over what was happening to her veterinary practice, she found herself laughing along with him.

He fell silent for a mile or so, and then shifted in the passenger seat to look at her. "You probably don't believe this, but I've never forgotten the night I stood you up at that Fourth of July celebration. I knew you'd be waiting there, the prettiest girl of all. And it tore me in two when I couldn't be there. I often wondered what might have happened between us if not for that night."

Surprised, she glanced at him before turning her attention back to the highway. The big holiday celebration drew people from all over the county for barbecue, watermelon, baking contests, and games for the children, and she'd been thrilled when Cole had offhandedly offered to meet her there. "I figured you just found somebody else that you wanted to be with that night."

"I—" He gave her a look of chagrin. "I always wished things could have been different."

The painful memory had never left her, either.

She'd spent hours trying to fix her hair and do her makeup, which had drawn extensive teasing from her sisters. She'd owned just three dresses—frippery, Claire had always said—and had tried each one on over and over, sure that none of them were pretty enough.

But when she and her family had arrived in town, Cole hadn't been there. She'd looked and looked, and had asked friends if they'd seen him. By the time the dance had started, and young and old alike had gathered, she'd caught the whispers and sly glances passing between the girls she'd thought were her friends.

In retrospect, perhaps those girls had been the daughters of ranch hands and other locals who just managed to get by, and they'd found the embarrassing fall of a McAllister girl to be especially delightful.

But the incident had wounded Leigh badly—both Cole's callous dismissal of her tender, young feelings, and the taunts that had followed her for months afterward. *Hey, Leigh, are you still looking for a boyfriend?* And *Must be tough. Guess being a McAllister doesn't make a difference, after all!*

She'd shoved those old hurts into the deepest recesses of her thoughts along with all of the other painful parts of her youth.

His words replayed through her mind. *It tore me in two when I couldn't be there.*

She flicked another glance at him. "I was so young then, so unsure. I never knew why you didn't show up. Did you have another date?"

His eyes were troubled. "Of course not. Something just…came up."

Realization spread a cold, unpleasant feeling through her midsection. "It was my mother," she said flatly. "I'll bet she called and told you to stay away from me."

He didn't answer.

"Did she? Did she threaten you?"

Cole's continuing silence confirmed her suspicions, and she slumped against the back of the seat, feeling defeated and empty. "It was such an innocent thing—wanting to walk around the Fourth of July celebration with you."

"Innocent?" His smile was sad and thoughtful. "Now that I have a young daughter, I'm seeing the other side of the fence. If Brianna wanted to see some wild young boy from a troubled family, I'd worry, too. And if she decided to meet him against my wishes, I'd probably ground her for a week. We want our children to be safe, Leigh. I don't think that's wrong, no matter how the kids feel at the time."

Leigh expected her answering smile was as sad as his own. "I know. And then Wes Truly was murdered and everything changed—for you and for me."

He reached over and touched her cheek. "I'm sorry."

"Old history, right? Just one of those things." At the Wilkinson ranch, she turned off the highway and drove down the long lane leading back into the foothills, where the barns and the house were set on a scenic rise overlooking the mountains.

This time, Ray Wilkinson didn't appear, but the gangly young cowhand did. He stood at the door of the main barn, then came out to meet them before they got out of the truck.

"Mr. Wilkinson ain't here," he said. Flags of high color brightened his cheeks and he didn't quite meet their eyes. "But he said…uh…that if you did come out, you weren't to stay."

"I hoped to examine the bull. To help your boss figure out why the animal died." She dipped her head, trying to meet the boy's eyes, but he just dropped his head lower.

"He'd want that, wouldn't he?" she continued. "To make sure his bull didn't die of some disease that the other cattle could get?"

The brim of the boy's hat came up a fraction. "He said he wasn't interested in…anything you had to say."

Cole leaned across the seat. "Can you tell us where your boss is? Or if he has a foreman around here somewhere?"

"Uh…I…"

At the sound of footsteps, he turned, his relief palpable.

Max strolled up and clapped him on the back, nodding toward the barn. "Go finish those stalls, son, I'll take care of this."

During their brief exchange, Leigh got out of the truck and Cole joined her. "I was asking the boy about me taking a look at that bull. I'm concerned, because it was in excellent condition when I left."

Max folded his arms, his feet planted wide, and shrugged. "Just following orders, here. The boss does not want you on this property, after what happened. He invested over twenty-thousand dollars in that animal."

"All the more reason to find out why it died."

Max smirked. "Ooooh, I think the boss has a pretty good idea. He's actually up in Jackson today, talking to his lawyers."

"He'll hardly have a leg to stand on in court without toxicology and necropsy reports," Cole said.

"That definitely won't be a problem. Another vet is already here."

"Can I talk to—"

"No." Max's eyes narrowed as he grabbed a cell phone clipped to his belt. "If you try to interfere, I was given orders to call in the law and have you arrested for trespassing. In fact, I'd like to see you try—I might enjoy seeing you two in handcuffs. It would sure look good if this came to trial."

Frustration welled in Leigh's throat. "Can you at least tell me who the vet is?"

Max snorted. "And let you try to influence him? I don't *think* so. Get out of here, before I call the law."

The likelihood that Michael or his deputies would really arrest her seemed slim to none, but risking additional problems with a legal case was another thing entirely.

She nodded to Cole. After he rounded her truck and got inside, she turned back to Max. "This is ridiculous. You know it is. That bull was in perfect condition when I left yesterday."

He gave her a look of smug satisfaction. "I'll deny ever saying it," he said in a low voice. "But payback is sweet, ain't it?"

She bit back the words that she knew she would regret later, and climbed behind the wheel of her truck. "I'm going to swing wide on my way out of here. See if you catch a glimpse of the other vet truck," she said to Cole.

"Got it."

She gave Max a casual wave and followed the perimeter of the parking area in front of the barns.

"I could just see the top of a truck and vet box. Gold, with the edges of what looks like black script across the side."

Leigh's heart sank. "This whole situation just gets worse and worse. I wouldn't be surprised if Max had something to do with that bull's death, because he just gloated about 'payback' after you were out of hearing range."

"He *what?*"

"And now Neil Adams is doing the necropsy. I don't even have to wait for the results before knowing that he'll probably 'find' something incriminating— because he really, really wants to see me fail."

During their trip back to the clinic, Brianna called Cole's cell phone and asked if she could come see the puppies when he and Leigh returned.

She arrived on her bike—after following the bumpy path from Cole's house—with two scraped knees and tears in her eyes.

Leigh had her hop up on an exam table and brought out a stainless-steel pan of warm, soapy water plus some sterile two-by-two gauze pads. "Do you want to do it, or should I?"

"You do it," Brianna whispered. "Please."

Cole peered over Leigh's shoulder as she began to gently cleanse the superficial wounds. "That must really hurt, honey. Maybe that bike isn't such a good idea out here."

"I could go out on the road." Brianna's face brightened. "That would be fun!"

"An eleven-year-old girl alone on a narrow, curvy, isolated highway? I don't *think* so."

"But I rode my bike on the street back home," she said, "Mom didn't mind."

"That was in a nice residential area. This is different." Cole rested a hand on Leigh's shoulder while she worked. A pleasant, friendly gesture, but Brianna's gaze flew between them and she frowned.

"Anyway," he continued, "it's a lot closer if you cut across the pasture, right?"

"I guess." The child flinched at the next touch of the gauze. "Can we go to the library today? You promised."

"You don't want to play with the puppies?"

"Not anymore. I'd rather get some books. Please?"

Leigh applied a mild triple-antibiotic cream, then covered each of Brianna's wounds with a wide adhesive bandage. "All set to go, young lady. Good as new!"

Cole gave Leigh's shoulder an extra little squeeze and stepped away. "Now you can tell all your friends that you go to a veterinarian, Bree," he teased.

She rolled her eyes at him and climbed off the table. "Can we go?"

He turned to Leigh. "You'll be all right here?"

"Of course. I don't expect you to be a bodyguard, and I certainly don't need one." She tipped her head toward the locked closet where she kept her shotgun. "You two run along."

There was concern in his eyes, but something else—a definite warmth that spoke of deepening feelings that matched her own. The realization made her pulse stumble.

He embraced her briefly, then held her at arm's length. "Call me if you have the least concern, okay? And don't hesitate to call 911, either."

She nodded, feeling a little dazed by his embrace…and she was still lost in that sensation long after he left.

A cautious, tender bud of joy began unfurling in her heart. Despite her statements to the contrary, it hadn't been just a foolish little infatuation that she'd felt for him all those years ago. She realized that now.

Her feelings had lain dormant. Silently waiting.

But being with him again had reawakened those feelings and made them bloom like wildflowers after a long drought.

Grinning, she suddenly realized her phone was ringing and hurried to pick it up—and probably sounded foolishly giddy when she answered.

The voice on the other end didn't sound nearly as happy.

"Leigh, this is Neil. Are you alone? We need to talk."

FOURTEEN

After some thought, Cole changed his mind about bringing Brianna along on this particular trip to town. A child in the room might temper what his quarry would be willing to say. If it didn't, she'd be hearing things no child her age should hear.

But when he drove from the clinic to his house to drop her off, her eyes filled with sudden tears.

"You *promised!*"

"I did, and I will follow through. But I've got business to take care of, and you'd be terribly bored. We'll go tomorrow for sure. Maybe even later today, if things work out. Okay?"

Her lower lip trembled. "You never want to spend time with me anymore," she cried as she jerked open her door and rushed up to the house.

Where had that come from? Mystified, he watched her disappear into the house and slam the door.

On the way to town, he tried to figure it out. Was it any easier for a woman to be a single parent of a young daughter? Half the time, he felt as if he were in a rudderless boat on stormy seas, and he had a hunch the next couple of years would be even more of a challenge.

He drove through town and headed out to Highway 12. At the second gravel road, he turned left and drove up to Don Miller's house—a small, shabby place with several junk cars parked in the drive.

He got out and rapped sharply on the door, which promptly aroused the ire of a small, beady-eyed dog standing on the back of a couch placed at the living-room window. It poked its nose through the curtains and started barking loud enough to wake the dead.

And also loud enough to alert its master, because after a good five minutes of nonstop noise, the face of an elderly man eventually appeared in the window, and then the front door opened slowly.

"I'm Cole Daniels. And I wonder—"

"I know who you are. Just go away and leave me be." Don slammed the door.

Cole knocked again, which started the dog off on a new round of crazed barking. Thanking the Lord for small favors, Cole waited until the dog quieted down, then knocked once more and started him up all over again.

The front door finally opened. "Don't you understand? I don't want you here!"

"Would you like to talk about your old friend, Gabe? I think it's mighty sad."

The man's bushy eyebrows drew together. "What?"

"You know that he died ten days ago."

"It was in the obituaries. So?"

"I talked to him that same afternoon. He seemed pretty healthy to me, but it was the strangest thing— he acted like he was afraid to talk to me. He made me shut the door for privacy, and even then he seemed really nervous when I started asking him questions. Isn't that odd?"

Don's gaze flickered. He took a step back, obviously intending to slam the door.

"I think someone threatened him. Sounds crazy, doesn't it? I mean, my dad took the fall for a murder he didn't commit. Now he's dead, so it's over and done with. I keep asking myself, why would it matter if any other version of the story surfaced? Who would care? But that answer is pretty obvious, don't you think?"

"I got nothing to say. Nothing at all."

Cole leaned a shoulder against the door frame, a subtle movement so the door couldn't slam shut. "A case could be made for obstruction of justice, I suppose. And you aiding and abetting a murderer isn't small potatoes, either, if it goes to trial. Are you willing to take that chance, Don?"

The man's mouth opened.

"There are only two of you left, now. Two of the men known to be a part of the poker game on the night Wes Truly died. You, Ed and Gabe were cleared of any potential murder charges back then. But there were others who were in that poker game, and I need their names."

Don's jaw hardened. "Don't remember."

"That's funny, because Gabe said the same thing. He seemed really nervous about it, too…but refusing to cooperate sure didn't seem to keep him from dying that night." Cole bared his teeth in a smile. "Did you know that his death was suspicious enough that the doctor ordered an autopsy?"

When Don didn't answer, Cole shrugged. "It seems to me that your best bet is telling me everything you know. Because if there's a killer on the loose, he just might come after you next. But if I can find him first, you might not have to worry."

"Like I told you, I got nothin' to say."

Cole drew a business card from his front pocket. "Here's my number. If you think of anything, contact either me or the sheriff. Just think—that one little call might save your life."

Neil showed up at Leigh's clinic in a half hour. He glanced around the waiting room, even though the lack of cars in the parking area should have been a good enough clue.

"There isn't anybody here, Neil," Leigh said. "So tell me—what's up?"

He paced the confines of the waiting room,

shoved a hand through his thinning hair. "It doesn't look good for you. Not at all. I've got to send those toxicology samples in as soon as I get to town, but from the looks of the bull's liver, they're going to find he was poisoned. There were petechiae in the esophagus, stomach and intestines, with generalized inflammation, so it's pretty clear that the substance was delivered orally. And with an animal that dangerous, it could only have been done while he was still restrained in the chute."

"Or when he was put back in it later," Leigh retorted. "I gave him nothing orally. No intravenous sedatives—just the appropriate amount of lidocaine to anesthetize the area. I sutured his wounds after thoroughly cleaning and debriding the tissues. And then I administered a loading dose of antibiotic intramuscularly—at the top of his hip. And that's it."

"Well, Wilkinson and his ranch hands are saying that you worked on that bull for a long time, and they didn't see everything you did. With their testimony in court, and your admitted presence at the ranch, Wilkinson figures he'll easily win a malpractice suit against you."

"That's crazy!"

"It's not only the purchase price of the animal. They bought him a couple years ago, and he was proving himself as a tremendous sire." Neil shook his head. "I can't even begin to imagine what they'll figure his worth is now."

"What are you getting at, Neil?"

He wouldn't look her in the eye. "I'm offering you a little deal. You know I once wanted our two practices combined into a partnership. I would have been willing to go fifty-fifty, though you weren't cooperative about that idea."

An ugly sensation crawled over her skin. "And now?"

"I'm thinking your license will be suspended over this. For sure, a lawsuit will far exceed any malpractice insurance coverage you have, which means you will lose everything."

"But I didn't do anything wrong."

"Good luck proving it—you were there, you worked on that bull. And with Wilkinson's high-powered lawyers, you won't stand a chance."

He was probably right, even if she didn't want to admit it.

Leigh closed her eyes, imagining how this might all play out. The humiliation. The damage to her reputation. The disbelief and disappointment in her mother's eyes. The financial aspect was just a small part of what this could mean to her future.

"What I'm saying," Neil continued, "is that I want to help you out."

She flinched.

"Of course, I can't switch samples. There's too much genetics work done on those bulls—someone might discover the discrepancy, if they check a little too closely. But they hauled the carcass off to a rendering plant after I finished the necropsy, so the samples I need to send in could be…compromised."

"As in?"

"Let me be concerned with that." Neil's voice grew smug. "In exchange, you could simply sign over my uncle's old practice for a nominal fee. That way, you could leave town and be free of all of this. No lawsuits, no damaged reputation."

She looked at him, incredulous. "I haven't even paid for the practice yet—beyond a down payment of ten grand from Uncle Gray, and my monthly payments."

"We'd have all the appropriate paperwork done, of course. I would assume the payments from here on out, once we completed the 'sale.' It's a good deal, Leigh. But it's also a now-or-never offer, because I need to ship those samples to the lab for analysis today."

She thought about the problems she'd faced over the past few months. "Tell me, Neil—just how bad have you wanted my practice? Did you flood the place? Write me a threatening letter? Or—"

He made a sharp motion with his hand. "Of course not. Why would I, when you were bound to mess things up, all on your own? I want that practice because I don't care to have any competition, and my own has far less potential. Owning both will solve all of that neatly, don't you think? My uncle should have just turned the practice over to me, and things would have been so much simpler."

If Neil was willing to tamper with evidence, he was also capable of lying to her about everything else, but it wasn't worth it to confront him.

She moved to the front door and opened it. "No deal, Neil. I'm going to leave my future in the hands of the Lord, because I did nothing wrong. And if you don't mind, I need to get back to work."

He went to the door, then turned back. "You know, I just made this offer as a favor—out of respect. When the Wilkinsons are through with you, you won't be able to show your face around these parts again, and then I'll be able to pick up your practice for a song. You've just made a very stupid mistake, sugar—and I promise you'll be sorry."

Leigh slumped into one of the waiting-room chairs feeling as if she'd just wrestled a dragon.

Neil had always made her feel uneasy. From day one, she'd sensed that he was less than honest. But the thought of him setting up such a complex deal based on a lie just took her breath away.

Would she lose her practice here, anyway?

That was a distinct possibility, if Neil was right about the testimony of Wilkinson and his ranch hands. She had no doubt that the man employed excellent lawyers.

Seeing her future dissipate before her eyes filled her with inestimable sadness. If Neil was right, she'd be lucky to find a clinic in another state that would even consider hiring her as an associate vet—and then, only after she passed that state's licensure exams.

After all these years, she and her sisters were starting to reconnect. She was trying to help with their mother, knowing that her advancing dementia would eventually mean even greater care. And then there was Cole....

But once she left Wolf Creek, it would all end.

At a slight knock at the door, she jerked upright in her chair and found Brianna peering inside.

"I thought you were going with your dad this afternoon," Leigh said wearily.

Brianna fidgeted in the doorway, then came in and sat in the seat across from Leigh's. "He said I couldn't 'cause he had to go talk to somebody. So I came back over on my bike."

"You look pretty sad."

"Yeah." Brianna eyed her with interest. "You look sorta sad, too. How come?"

"I—I'm just thinking about the future. Life isn't always easy." Leigh dredged up a smile. "But enough about that. Are you here to play with the puppies?"

"Yeah." Her face brightened. "And I had some *great* news about my mom and dad!"

Leigh blinked. "Really?"

"They talk and talk on the phone every night, about how they want to be back together. Like a *real* family. And I think it's going to happen really soon!"

"*Really.*" Leigh swallowed. "How... How wonderful for you."

Brianna bounced out of her chair. "I know. Isn't it awesome?"

Leigh watched her flit back to the kennel area, radiating such joy that the air seemed to sing with it. What would it be like to ever be that happy, even for a moment?

It was too impossible to even consider.

Whatever she'd imagined about Cole's touch, or about the feelings in the depths of his beautiful eyes, had all just been her foolish thoughts...unless he was a man who didn't mind casual flirtations on the side when his true love was off in another state.

Either way, there'd never really been a chance for the happiness she'd once dreamed of...but what did she expect?

Feeling as if things just couldn't get any worse today, she stood and went back to check on Brianna.

And then the phone rang.

FIFTEEN

"I talked to Don Miller," Cole said over the phone.

Still dazed after her meeting with Neil, Leigh drew a blank. "Who?"

"He was at the tavern the night of the murder."

"And?"

Cole paused. "You sound different. Is something wrong?"

"I'm okay—just had a little discussion with Neil, but I'll tell you later." She tried to dredge up more enthusiasm. "Did Don—um—tell you what you needed to know?"

"Not at first. But after Michael told me about Gabe's autopsy report, I called Don to let him know about it, just to see what he would say. I think it shook him, because he agreed to talk to me. I'm on my way out there now."

Feeling as if she were at the back of the pack in a long race, she tried to follow. "Back up a minute. What about Gabe?"

"Just as I thought, he didn't die of natural causes. He was suffocated."

Leigh drew in a sharp breath. "That poor man."

"Michael and his deputies are at the care center now, interviewing the staff and residents. They asked me to come over because I was the last visitor to see him. I found something interesting—several names in the guest book."

"Any suspects?"

"Perhaps. Gabe was frightened about talking to me, so someone must have warned him to keep quiet. Several familiar names stood out—Don Miller, Ed Quinton and Lowell Haskins, though I don't know if that means anything. The receptionist made me a copy of those pages before she turned the book over to the deputies."

"They were all ranch hands, far as I know. I don't remember any of them having reputations for serious trouble."

"Something just doesn't seem right about all of this. I'm missing some detail, some connection, and I can't quite see it."

"Be careful, Cole. Maybe you should leave this up to the sheriff's office."

"I know I'm no cop—I'm just trying to clear my father's name. I'm pulling into Don's driveway now, and I'll let Michael know right away if he says anything significant. Afterward, I'll to try to find Ed Quinton one last time."

"He's the one who lives in town, right?"

"Supposedly. I've stopped by several times, but never found him home."

Leigh disconnected the call and drifted through her temporary clinic, feeling at a complete loss.

At the clinic in town, she'd had small-animal appointments. Drop-ins that had helped fill the day. But with the Wilkinson situation and her more isolated location, things were going from bad to worse.

She stared out the windows toward the mountains, her usual awe at those glorious peaks dimmed. How could something that had started out so well, with such hope, be ending so terribly wrong?

Her monthly payments on her various loans were coming due in two weeks, and there was no way she could pay them.

Choking back the emotions building in her throat, she stared up at the mountains and then closed her eyes. *I don't know what You want for me, Lord. Was this move back to Wyoming a mistake? Please help me to see the right path in all of this because I just don't know which way to turn.*

After Brianna left for home, Leigh wandered through the clinic, cleaning and sorting supplies, feeling more empty than she ever had before. Even Hobo looked sad as he limped along behind her.

When the phone jangled an hour later, she startled at the unexpected noise.

"I've got a colic," a male voice said. "We're out about fifteen miles south of Wolf Creek. Take a left by the abandoned house, then follow that lane to the end. *Hurry.*"

"On my way," she replied. "What's your name and number?"

"Peterson." He rattled off a number that she jotted on a clipboard. "We just moved here from Colorado, so we aren't in the phone book. My sister works in the bank, though. You've probably met her."

"Karen or Julie?"

"That's right—Karen."

Her heart feeling lighter, Leigh hurried out to her truck, threw a jacket in the back seat and hit the road, drumming her fingers on the steering wheel in time to a country-western song on the radio.

As an afterthought, she dialed Cole's cell phone and left her destination on his voice mail, then she floored the accelerator across the vast open plains that spread from the foothills to the eastern horizon.

A sudden rustling movement in the back seat sent her heart straight up her throat.

She stepped hard on the brakes. Looking up at the rearview mirror, she found Brianna staring back at her, her eyes round and face pale.

Relief rushed through her, followed by exasperation. "What on earth are you doing in here, young lady?"

Brianna's eyes widened even more, then she sat

back and slumped down in the seat. "I—I needed to talk to somebody."

"Why didn't you come into the clinic?"

"I...um...thought you might b-be too busy or that you'd be mad and make me go home," she said miserably. "And then Dad would be mad, too. I almost did come in, but..."

"You overheard me talking on the phone?"

"I didn't *mean* to." She sniffled. "It just sorta happened, and I knew you'd be leaving. I thought if I came along, you'd have to listen longer."

Leigh had a sudden insight about what the child was trying to say. "This wouldn't have anything to do with your story about your mom and dad, would it?"

"I...I..." Brianna started to cry. "I keep telling Dad that we should invite Mom here. For a nice visit, so they can make up. B-but...then I heard him talking to Mom on the phone before I came over. He was really mad, and h-he—"

Oh, dear. "Brianna, if you overheard something, you were only hearing half the conversation. You need to talk this over with your dad so he can explain."

"He was mad 'cause she didn't want me to come back for my long v-visit. He said I should be more important th-than anything else. Then she must've hung up on him, 'cause he just stood there with his eyes closed, holding the phone at his side. He looked so *angry.*"

Please, Lord, help me say the right thing to this

poor child. "Everyone has disagreements, sweetheart."

"I just want things back like they were, so we'd be a family again. If I'd been better and hadn't been so much trouble, maybe…" She hiccupped.

"Honey, parents don't break up because of something their kids do. They *love* their kids, and the last thing they want is to be separated from them. Divorce is all about the grown-ups."

The child broke into a fresh round of sobs. "A-and now Mom doesn't even want me with her."

"*Every* mother loves her children with her whole heart. Maybe your mom just had a conflict with work, or something." Unsure if Brianna was taking the reassurance to heart, Leigh wanted to pull over and comfort her. She *definitely* wanted to turn around and take her home.

But with just a few miles left to the location of the colic case, that extra time could mean the difference between life and death for the animal.

"Look, I need to let your dad know where you are, and I need to treat a sick horse. But after I get done with this call, we'll talk for as long as you want. Okay?"

Through the rearview mirror, Leigh saw Brianna nod.

"Okay then…I think I see the turn just ahead." Leigh called and left another message for Cole, then shoved her cell phone into the clip on her belt.

"Your dad must be busy, but at least he'll know where you are."

She turned onto a dusty lane leading out into the sagebrush. It wound around a ravine, down into a gully, then back up the other side. "Wow. These people recently moved here, but they sure haven't fixed their road yet."

At the top of the next rise, she pulled to a stop. Ahead lay a steep downward slope. And as far as the eye could see, there were low, rolling hills of sand and sagebrush, without a building in sight. An uneasy premonition crawled down her spine.

"It's time to turn around," she said, keeping her voice calm. "Maybe the guy gave me the wrong directions."

But she'd followed them exactly.

And they'd led exactly nowhere.

Grabbing her clipboard, she dialed the phone number the man had given her.

After eight rings, an elderly woman answered, but her confusion over Leigh's call was obvious.

Making a quick three-point turn, Leigh headed back toward the highway, going a little faster this time; angry at herself for believing the caller, even though such farm visits were a daily occurrence as a large-animal vet. Had this been some stupid prank—some high-school kid just having a lark?

Grasping that possibility, she breathed a little easier.

From now on, she would do a callback on every single ranch appointment, to verify the person and location. This had been a very foolish mistake. And worse—Cole's daughter was with her. What if—

With her next heartbeat, *what if* became chilling reality.

She drew in a sharp breath and slammed on the brakes at the bottom of the gully.

"What is it?" Brianna leaned over the front seat, her voice strained. "Is something wrong?"

"Get down, fast," Leigh hissed. "Do as I say. Now!"

Brianna started to whimper.

"And be totally *quiet.* Cover yourself with that old blanket, and do not move. Is that clear? No matter what you see or hear, not one peep."

"P-promise," the girl whispered, her voice trembling.

Brianna couldn't have seen it from the back seat, but ahead of them, at the top of the gully rim, a big, black Ford truck was parked across the road.

And the driver stood next to it, silhouetted by the setting sun, with a rifle at his side. With a single, fluid motion, he raised the weapon to his shoulder, took careful aim…

And fired.

This time, it didn't take a dog alarm to bring Don Miller to the door.

He'd apparently put the noisy little beast in a back room, and was surreptitiously watching at the window when Cole arrived. After opening the front door, he carefully scanned his cluttered yard before slamming the door and ramming the dead bolt home.

"Is someone else coming?" Cole asked.

The old man shuffled over to an old recliner, reached for a shotgun leaning against the wall and sat with it lying across his lap. "I hope not."

"Should I be worried about that weapon of yours?"

Don snorted. "This ain't about you. But if there's any trouble, I'd recommend you get out of the way. Fast."

Cole looked for a place to sit among the stacks of old newspapers and cardboard boxes. The little house had been cluttered before, but now it was even worse. He shifted a cardboard box from the faded sofa to a stack on the coffee table. "You've been busy. Are you cleaning, or moving?"

"Traveling. I got relatives someplace else."

"Would this have anything to do with Gabe's death?"

Don swore under his breath. "What do you think?"

"Maybe you can fill me in this time. I think I can help."

"And how would you do that?" he snarled. "You're not armed, and you're not a cop. You just want to clear your daddy's name, and then you'll be gone. I won't last a day, if I help you."

"You will, if the law gets a chance to nail the guy who's responsible. And since you obviously know who he is, maybe we can get down to business."

Don nodded. "You probably know your dad was quite a brawler in his day. Drank heavy, fought hard. Had a quicksilver temper, Rand did." Don stopped on a wheezy cough. "A good man—don't get me wrong. More talent on them cutting horses than anyone I ever saw. But you never wanted to cross him if he had a bottle in his hand, and he never forgot a grudge. Him and Gray McAllister had one that went way back over some horse deal that went sour."

The man was rambling, and the minutes were ticking by. Cole suppressed the urge to glance at his watch. "So when did you arrive at the tavern? Were you there the entire evening?"

"Longer than I ever should have been. Worst mistake I ever made, showing up that night. Learned my lesson, though. Never picked up another card. Ever."

"Were you there before Wes Truly showed up?"

Don stared at the ceiling, as if his thoughts were traveling back in time. "I usually got there at eight o'clock. Maybe nine. He was at the bar, acting like he'd already had too much. When a group of ranch hands walked in looking for excitement on a Saturday night, he asked if anybody was up for a little fun. Wasn't long and a couple guys lost everything they had in their pockets. The others—me, Rand, Ed and Gabe—were in too deep to quit."

"Who dropped out of the game early?"

"Some I didn't know—a couple new guys from the Bellman ranch. Then there was Fred Young, Haskins and his cousin, and someone named Tate— don't remember his last name. Never saw him again, and I don't know where he came from. Some guys thought he was in cahoots with Wes, but once the fight broke out, he disappeared. Of course, a lot of other guys ran—didn't want to risk a run-in with the law. They—"

The phone on the side table next to his recliner rang.

Don paled. He started to reach for it, his hand hovering like a frightened bird over the receiver.

"Are you going to answer that?"

He'd been on a pretty good roll, reliving the details Cole had hoped for. Now, his mouth worked without him saying anything at all.

"Maybe you'd better. If it's private, I can leave the room."

The receiver shook as Don brought it to his ear. He'd been pale before, but as he silently listened, his face turned dead-white.

A moment later, he dropped the receiver back into the cradle.

Unless Cole missed his guess, the caller was the one who had threatened Gabe Brown, and quite possibly was responsible for his death. "Who was it?"

Gripping the shotgun, Don lumbered to his feet

and disappeared down the hallway. He returned a moment later with a small dog carrier and headed straight for the front door.

"Wait—don't just run!" Cole followed him outside to a battered Chevy pickup. "Tell me who it was. Let me call the sheriff."

Don silently loaded the dog carrier and shotgun into the front seat of the truck, then climbed in after them and settled behind the wheel. "I already said too much, and I'm not getting killed over this. Understand?"

"You'll be safer if you stay. Don't you get it? Run, and you'll always be watching your back."

The motor roared to life. "I gave you what you needed, now get out of my way."

He threw the truck in reverse, swung around, then sped down the drive in a cloud of dust.

Cole started for his own vehicle, then stopped and looked back at the house. The door was wide open. If Don had caller ID, it might yield everything Cole wanted to know.

If there was time. The guy who'd called a few minutes ago could be on his way right now—planning to find Don and terminate yet one more risk.

Pulling out his cell phone, Cole noticed the symbol indicating voice mail, but there wasn't time to check it now.

He hit the speed-dial button for Michael's cell. Told him about the mysterious caller and Don's sudden departure, asked for help, then he raced back to the telephone in the living room. There was no caller ID.

He lifted the receiver. Dialed *69 to hear the phone number of that last caller and jotted it down on a scrap of paper as he let the number dial on through.

No one answered. Without a caller-ID screen or a handy computer for a quick reverse phone-number lookup, he had no idea who he'd just called.

But then Don's words rolled through his mind once more. *I gave you what you needed.*

And suddenly, everything fell into place.

SIXTEEN

Leigh froze when the first bullet hit her truck.

By the time the second one hit, she'd wrenched the wheel, stomped on the gas and careened into a tight turn.

If the shooter hit a tire, she and Brianna might never make it out of this isolated place…and she definitely wasn't waiting around to see what the man had to say.

"Get your seat belt on—but stay down!" Leigh ordered. "And hurry."

The truck bounced wildly over the bumpy, narrow track, going airborne over the deeper ruts, then landing with teeth-jarring force.

Brianna, bless her heart, had to be enduring a rough ride in the back seat, but she was safer there—protected by the bulk of the vet box in the bed of the truck.

At the top of the last rise, Leigh hesitated for a split second, and looked back. Dust boiled up behind the truck pursuing them…. He was maybe a half mile back, and he was gaining ground. *Please Lord, tell me where to go—what to do.* Her shotgun was cradled in the gun rack above the back seat of the truck, but the last thing she needed was a gun battle—and her pursuer had far greater range with his rifle.

She hesitated, then stepped on the gas, hit the bottom of the hill and took a sharp right, praying even harder as she sped over the rockier ground and tried to avoid the larger outcroppings that could tear at the gas tank and exhaust system underneath.

But at least there was far less dust here…less evidence of where she was. And with the lay of the land, she'd be out of sight in seconds.

If the other truck went the wrong way, it would give her precious seconds to double back. "Hold on, Brianna—we're going to be okay. I promise!"

Just ahead, a deep cut in the landscape abruptly opened up and she spun the steering wheel to the right, threw the truck into four-wheel drive and started the sharp ascent.

The vehicle launched over the top rim of the slope, went airborne once again, then slammed to the ground and swayed wildly, the tires spinning in soft, sandy ground.

Behind her, the black pickup suddenly filled her rearview mirror.

Her wheels hit bottom in the sand, caught against solid ground, and the truck rocketed forward toward the county highway that promised a fast trip back to civilization.

A mile… Half mile… A few hundred yards…

Someone had closed a heavy pipe gate across the lane. Thick chains were padlocked to the cement posts at either end.

Did she dare go through it? The gate could break free, or hitting it could mean the impact of a head-on collision. But if she stopped, she had no doubt about what her pursuer intended.

An endless litany of prayer rushed through her mind as she aimed for the three-strand barb-wire fence to the left of the gate…and prayed her truck could make it through.

"Hold on, honey—we're almost there!"

On impact, the truck jerked, whiplashing her forward, then back. Then the wires snapped and the truck lurched through, only to skid sideways and tip wildly on two wheels before righting itself.

The truck behind them was close—too close. It veered to avoid a collision with her bumper—and with a deafening crash it hit the cement post broadside.

Stunned and shaking, Leigh angled up out of the ditch to the highway and drove a dozen yards before slowing and looking back.

The driver's side of the other truck was T-boned around the post, and the sunlight highlighted something wet and dark trailing down the crumpled door. The driver, just a dim, shadowed form inside, wasn't moving.

"Brianna—honey. Are you all right?" Leigh wrenched her cramped fingers from the steering wheel and twisted in her seat.

The child looked blankly at her, her eyes huge and dark in contrast to her pale face. "I—I think so." Her lower lip trembled and her eyes filled with tears. "I-is it over? Can we go home?"

"You bet. Soon—really soon."

Leigh fumbled in her purse for her cell phone and flipped it open. She dialed 911 for the sheriff and an ambulance. Then noticed that sometime in the last ten minutes Cole had returned her call without leaving a message.

She looked back at the black truck, torn with doubt. The driver was no friend, but if he wasn't dead already, he might be hurt badly enough to bleed to death by the time the ambulance arrived. Yet Brianna was with her—and did she dare risk Brianna's safety for the life of someone who'd wished them both dead?

She hesitated, then stepped out of the truck, took her shotgun out of its rack and kissed Brianna's forehead. "The sheriff and ambulance are on their way. And earlier, I told your dad where I was, so I'd guess he's on his way, too. I've got to go see if I can help that man."

Her words seemed to snap Brianna out of her

stupor. "No!" she screamed, clutching at Leigh with both hands. "Please, no!"

Leigh carefully extricated herself from the child's grip. "I'm locking the truck, and I want you to stay low. Don't unlock it for anyone but your dad or Michael, understand?"

"P-please!"

"I've got my shotgun, and I'll be careful. I—I just can't stand here and let someone die."

Leigh hit the locks and slammed the door shut, the image of Brianna's terrified expression still clear in her mind as she crouched low and ran along the ditch until she was even with the gate.

She peered across the road.

Through the front window, she could see the man's head leaning against the steering wheel, and his left arm dangling out the window, as still as death.

She checked to make sure the shotgun was loaded. Then she lifted it to her shoulder and aimed it at the windshield as she crept across the road, never taking her eyes off the driver's inert form.

Circling the truck from the back, she moved in closer. Blood dripped from the man's shoulder to his fingertips, and fell to a dark, slick pool on the ground. A collapsed airbag draped over the steering wheel beneath the man's head, a wash of crimson blood garish against the white plastic.

"Sir? Are you okay?"

He didn't move.

"Sir? I'm here to help you. The sheriff and ambulance are on the way, and should be here any minute."

She got a little closer. Watched. Then, with her right hand still ready at the trigger of the shotgun, she edged another few inches and, holding her breath, peered inside. He was facing the other way.

She cautiously reached for the wrist dangling outside the door to check for a pulse.

Like a rattlesnake, he jerked back, caught the barrel of the shotgun and threw her off balance, then grabbed her hair in a viselike grip. The shotgun fell to the ground.

"I figured you'd waltz over here, sooner or later," he snarled. "A bleeding heart like you is just too easy."

The moment she heard his voice, sixteen years of nightmares slammed back into her head.

Mayhem had erupted outside the tavern on the night of Wes Truly's murder.

People had been running everywhere. Shouting.

Some had lit out for the parking lot, others had crowded around Rand Daniels, who'd been pinned to the ground by three burly ranchers.

But *this* was the voice of the man who'd seen her. Who had loomed close to Uncle Gray's truck, his face masked by the low brim of his hat, to deliver a warning.

The sheriff had discounted the mysterious stranger as a buddy of Rand's who had probably been trying to protect his friend. The fact that Rand himself was caught with the knife had been deemed indisputable evidence.

Now, she tried to wrench free of his grasp, but the man twisted his hand in her hair and lifted a handgun, aiming it in her direction.

"I figure…" He coughed, sending a fine spray of blood spattering against the steering wheel. "You and me will go for a ride. Your truck oughta work just fine."

She blinked away the black spots dancing in front of her eyes. There was no way she could let him get near her truck and Brianna.… No way, no matter what the cost.

A cost that would probably be measured in minutes because she knew that one way or the other, he wouldn't let her walk away alive.

"Th-they'll find out who you are. They'll trace this truck."

"A stolen truck? Won't matter now, will it?" His laugh was harsh. "Too bad you and your friend had to come back to Wyoming and start nosing around. You both would have lived a lot longer."

She struggled, trying to get a good look at his face.

But she knew without a doubt that it was *him*.

Her stomach roiling, she abruptly let her knees buckle, so his injured arm held her entire weight.

He screamed in agony and fired.

The bullet went wild, shattering the windshield.

But at that instant, she broke free, scooped up her shotgun and took aim at his head. "Believe me, I *know* I have nothing to lose. You toss that gun on the floor. One wrong move and you'll have a split second left to live."

Cole arrived minutes later.

After a quick look at the situation, he helped Leigh move Lowell to the ground, then found the handgun in the black pickup and kept it trained on the man's chest. Leigh stopped the bleeding with pressure and bandaging materials from her truck.

"This must be Lowell Haskins," Cole said grimly. "Just the man I wanted to find."

Leigh's eyes widened. "This is *Lowell?* He's been a terrifying nightmare of mine ever since the night of the murder. He ran past my uncle's truck and scared me half to death, but I couldn't see his face. I recognize the voice though."

Surprised, Cole looked at her. "You don't know him? I thought he worked for your mother."

"Not while I lived there. He's vaguely familiar, so I probably saw him around town or at a rodeo a few times as a kid. But a lot of ranch hands come and go in the area, and I rarely ever got to town."

When the ambulance and deputy's patrol car arrived, Cole and Leigh stepped back.

"Brianna's still in my truck," Leigh whispered, her voice trembling. She was shaking now, and couldn't seem to stop. "She's been through quite a lot during the last hour or so."

"And she *should* have been at home the whole time." Cole turned and found Brianna staring out the window in awe at the emergency vehicles. He waved and held up a finger, indicating he'd be over in a minute. "She and I will be having a talk one of these days about obedience."

The deputy—Joe Paulson—hovered with a clipboard and pen, talking to Lowell as the EMT team got him settled on a stretcher. As soon as it was loaded, the vehicle left with lights and sirens.

"They said you refused to be examined," Joe said, glancing at Leigh and then frowning at his notes. "Are you sure you're all right?"

"Cole's daughter and I were lucky—probably just a few bumps. It could have been so much worse."

"Can I speak with her, too?"

"She didn't see much, but if it's all right with her father…"

Cole nodded and went to get Brianna. She was obviously nervous over the first questions, then became more animated about the wild ride she'd had with a really, *really* bad man in pursuit.

"I'm taking her home," Cole said after the deputy finished. "Where will you be, Leigh?"

She raised an eyebrow at the deputy, who

shrugged. "I just have a few more questions, ma'am, and then I'll let you go. Sheriff Robertson will be contacting you very soon, I'm sure."

Exhausted but too nervous to rest, Leigh went home for a quick shower, then headed up to Cole's house where he met her on the porch. His house-keeper, Polly, came out and made a big fuss over her, offering her lemonade and cookies, but after bringing out the refreshments, she tactfully with-drew to another part of the house.

Leigh toyed with her glass. "I can't believe what happened today. It keeps playing over and over in my mind, like some crazy cartoon or show on TV. These things just don't happen to a small-town vet."

"Not unless there's somebody after them with a vendetta and not much to lose."

"But *Lowell?*" She shook her head in disbelief. "I knew there was a lot of friction between him and my mother. But who would've guessed he'd go this far?"

"After Don left town, I went looking for Ed Quinton. I found him at his son's house. He hadn't been back at his own place for weeks. When you and I moved back to town, Lowell got nervous. And when he heard that I was asking a lot of questions, he must have gotten *scared*. All those years, getting away with murder—then the wrong people show up."

"I still don't understand."

"Don gave me the first lead. He told me the names of the men who left that poker game early, and Haskins was one of them. His name also appeared on the guest book at the care center." Cole gave her a wry smile. "When I told Ed what I knew, and about what happened to Gabe, he couldn't stop talking.

"Lowell was livid after losing hundreds of dollars, but when Truly drew a gun, he backed off. For the rest of the night, he must have been waiting in the shadows for Truly to come out."

"So your father was just in the wrong place at the wrong time. He must not have been thinking right when he picked up that knife. He was probably in shock, after coming outside and finding somebody bleeding to death."

"And since only his fingerprints were on the knife, Lowell must have been wearing gloves."

They both fell silent over the enormity of what had happened, both in the past and today.

"I just can't tell you how horrible I feel about all of this. I—I testified at your dad's trial. I helped send the wrong man to prison. Because of me…" A knot formed in her throat and she felt her eyelids burn. "I am just so sorry—so terribly sorry, Cole. I just wish I could turn back the clock, because I won't ever be able to forgive myself for this."

Cole covered her hand with his own. "You described what you saw, Leigh, and the other witnesses did, too. All the evidence just pointed in the wrong direction."

"But still…"

He shook his head. "It isn't your fault. You told the truth as you knew it. I've spent far too many years assuming the worst about everyone involved. It got me exactly nowhere, and I finally realized that I simply had to give it all over to God. The blame rests squarely on Lowell's shoulders. Not yours."

She'd spent those same years dwelling on uncertainty and self-recrimination, and his words lifted some of that weight from her chest. "Thank you," she said quietly. "Though it's going to take a long time for me to accept that."

"Lowell probably killed Gabe, too," he added. "Just compounding his sins, one after another. You and my daughter were going to be next."

Leigh shuddered.

Cole squeezed her hand. "I just can't imagine losing either of you. This whole situation has made me realize just how much I care about you, Leigh. I swore I'd never take another chance after what Alicia did, but…I'd sure like to try."

She studied him sadly, thinking that he was one of the kindest, most honorable men she'd ever met. He was a loving father and just being with him made her feel whole. What would it be like to marry a man like Cole, and have a fairy-tale, happily-ever-after ending in her life?

"Just so you know, your daughter was in my truck because she wanted to talk to me, and thought she'd have more time if she snuck along on a vet call. She…wanted to apologize."

"For what?"

"She…told me earlier that you and your ex-wife have been talking frequently, and that you'll get together again soon. I think she's afraid you'll connect with someone new, and that scares her."

"That's beyond wishful thinking, imagining her mother and I would ever reunite. Alicia was engaged just months after she left me, and now she's got everything she ever wanted."

"I thought as much. But Brianna's feeling threatened and scared, and I…. Well, maybe it's time for a little more space. I'm calling the contractors tomorrow, to see if I can move back to my clinic in town. Maybe they can just sort of work around me while they finish up. Otherwise, I can probably find another building in town, somewhere."

His eyes widened. "You want to *leave?*"

"I think it would be better this way, don't you?" A deep feeling of loss enveloped her heart. "The way things are going, I might not have my practice much longer, anyhow. So who knows where I'll be in a few months? It might be best to cut the connection now."

"Of course." His eyes cooled, grew distant as he

met her gaze. "Don't worry about making that move. I'll have my hired hands take care of it as soon as you know where you're going."

SEVENTEEN

On Monday, Leigh was slowly putting supplies back on the shelves of Doc Adams's old clinic when Michael stopped by. "We missed you at dinner on Sunday," he said. "Janna tried to call, but didn't get an answer."

Leigh wearily rested her palms at the small of her back. "I talked to the contractor on Saturday afternoon. He said I could start moving back here, even though the waiting room isn't quite finished. The paneling still needs to be replaced out there, and some of the vinyl-floor tiling buckled, so it still has to be redone."

"You don't look very excited. Do you want us to come over and help? Janna and I could come tonight, if you need us."

"I guess I've just lost heart over this whole deal. I was so excited about moving back to Wolf Creek. I love the area, and really wanted to be close to my family. But there's been one problem after another, and I'm not sure it's financially feasible to stay."

Michael smiled. "Sounds like I came at a good time. What would you like first, the good news or the really good news?"

"At this point, I don't even know. Is it something about Lowell Haskins?"

"Yes, but it goes beyond the Wes Truly murder case. He probably would have gotten away with it, but he made a lot of mistakes, and some of them have affected you. Someone is stopping by in a few minutes who wants to make things right for you."

"It may be too late for that." She waved a hand toward the empty waiting room. "You know the verse in Ecclesiastes about a good reputation being more valuable than costly perfume? I no longer have time to salvage mine. I'm going to have to sell the practice just so I can clear as many of my debts as possible."

"Don't be so sure." He handed her a folder. "I think you'll be surprised to find just how far Haskins went to protect his secrets. Once he was released from the ER, I took him down to the county jail on two counts of first-degree murder, for starters. He has been remarkably cooperative—but maybe carrying all that guilt was harder than just letting it go."

"So, do you have a tight case against him—or is he going to be back out on the street in six months?"

The laugh lines at the corners of Michael's eyes deepened. "One bad thing about being a bully is that you don't have many loyal friends. Now that he's behind bars, the people he intimidated are more than happy to talk. He's the one who's been intimidating you, hoping you'd just leave town. No doubt he was afraid that if you ever ran into him on the street, you'd remember seeing him on the night of the murder."

"Is that why he didn't show up for the job interview at Cole's?"

"Probably. We now know that he's the one who damaged your sprinkler system, and we're pretty sure he's the one who poisoned Wilkinson's bull."

Leigh rocked back on her heels, surprised. "I was sure that was Max. He seemed so delighted to see me take the blame for that. My second thought was Neil, because he was ready to capitalize on that bull's death the minute he heard about it."

"Actually, Lowell and Max are buddies from way back. Wilkinson thinks Max probably fully cooperated in the bull's death, and he's pressing charges against both of them. I can only imagine the hefty lawsuits he'll level against those men, but with Lowell's future in prison he'll never earn enough money to pay restitution."

Someone knocked on the back door of the clinic and strolled in. She turned and saw Cole standing in the hallway, holding his western hat at his side.

"Have you told her?" he asked.

"Not yet. I was just trying to make sure she knew what was happening with Lowell first."

She looked between the two men, her curiosity rising. "Is there something else I should know?"

"Just that you need to come outside for a minute."

She looked down at her dusty shirt and faded jeans. "I'm kind of busy. Can we do this later?"

Cole laughed. "I don't think so." He tilted his head toward the back door. "Come on back and take a look."

Mystified, she whistled for Hobo, then walked outside, the dog following at her heels. Cole and Michael were right behind her.

Standing out in the sunshine was Ray Wilkinson, dressed in a suit, talking to several people with microphones. A small crowd had gathered—people she recognized from town—and to the side, Janna, Rylie, Brianna, Tessa and even her mother were standing together. Michael walked over to them and draped an arm around Janna's shoulders.

Wilkinson looked over and nodded to Leigh, then unfolded a piece of paper and began reading. "I just wanted to publicly apologize for any misconceptions that might have arisen from the loss of one of my bulls. I know rumors are flying about our new vet, Dr. Leigh McAllister. I have no doubt that these rumors have hurt her professionally and personally, and I'd like to repair that damage in any way I can. She responded to an emergency call at our ranch promptly, and provided the best of care. Our bull died due to the actions of a trespasser and one of my former employees. Legal actions are pending against the men responsible.

"If Dr. McAllister is still willing to provide services for my livestock, I plan to continue to fully utilize the services of the Wolf Creek Veterinary Clinic. And because of my full confidence in her, I plan to discuss the possibility of keeping her on retainer to affirm our association. I'd also like to offer her a no-interest loan to help ensure that Wolf Creek Veterinary Services will have a solid future for all of us who have animals in need of high-quality care."

A smattering of applause broke out in the crowd, then the people began to chat with each other. Some started for the cars parked down the road. Others headed her way, offering good wishes and promises that they would be bringing their animals to her clinic in the future.

When the townspeople finally dispersed, Cole leaned close to Leigh. "Smart man," he whispered. "I'll bet Wilkinson's lawyers warned him that you could sue over the things he said about you, so he just made a public apology. I also think you'll be hearing an apology from another one of your 'friends' shortly. When Wilkinson announced to the media that he wanted coverage today, one of the reporters commented to me that her own vet was saying negative things about you as well."

"That would be Neil," Leigh said dryly. "Professional to the bone, and he is *such* a nice guy."

"Michael went over to Salt Grass and set him straight…warned him about the legal consequences he could face. If you want to, you could file a no-contact order against him to avoid any further awkward scenes."

That made her laugh. "Like, his offer to tamper with legal evidence? The promises that he's going to swoop in and nab my practice when I flounder?"

"He's the one who's floundering, from what I hear." A muscle ticked at the side of Cole's jaw. "I think I may have a talk with him myself."

"I wouldn't want to hurt his reputation with that no-contact deal. But if he shows up again, I'll lay things on the line so even he can understand." She grinned, feeling stronger and more assured than she ever had, as she absorbed the warm smiles of the people who had come here today—friends and family and members of her church. People who cared enough to show up. It felt so *good* to be home. "I have a feeling things are going to be a lot better, from now on."

"I hope so, because you deserve it." He gave her hand a quick squeeze. "I suppose I'd better get back home. I've got a half-dozen training horses now, so things are getting busy out at my place."

"I'm glad," she murmured. "Remind Brianna that she's welcome to come to the clinic anytime, if she'd like."

She watched Cole walk to his truck and drive away, her momentary joy fading.

"You look like you just lost your best friend." Janna strolled up to Leigh and gave her a quick hug. "Not such a great day after all?"

"Of course it is. I couldn't be happier."

"If that's happy, I sure don't want to see you when you're sad," Claire snorted.

Leigh turned and smiled at her mother, taking in the deep lines of her face—the road map of a hard and bitter life—and wondered if there'd ever been a time when Claire had been truly content.

Before her early marriages? Before widowhood and the stresses of raising small children alone while competing in a man's world?

"What makes you happy, Mama?" Leigh murmured. The words were out before she could call them back. "After all you've been through, and the changes you've faced in your life, is there anything left that really brings you joy?"

It was a crazy question, directed to a woman who'd no more dwell on emotions than she would deign to perform somersaults across the parking lot.

But a rare glimmer of humor briefly touched Claire's mouth. "The right man did once," she said. "Until he up and died on me. That was your daddy."

"And after that?"

"My girls."

That answer surprised Leigh so much that her

mouth fell open. Never, even in her most distant memories, had there ever been a hint. Then again, maybe it was just Claire's dementia talking.

"You think I didn't love you. But I know how cruel the world is. How it can rip away your happiness. How it takes away the ones you love. Now look at yourself and tell me—didn't you learn to work till you drop? To have a tough skin? Did you give up on your biggest dreams, or did you make them happen?"

Leigh stared at her, stunned. In all her years, Claire had rarely given more than monosyllabic answers. And she'd never, ever hinted at the fact that somewhere, beneath that crusty exterior, lay a warm and beating heart.

"I—" Leigh floundered, searching for the right answer. "I understand," she said finally.

And hours later, as she sat at her bedroom window with Hobo curled at her feet, she did. "Hey, buddy," she said. "Would you like to go for a ride?"

On the way out to Four Winds Ranch, Leigh started second-guessing her decision. Debated. Nearly turned around. It was already ten o'clock. Maybe it was too late to stop out there. Maybe everyone was already asleep.

Maybe it was the dumbest thing she'd ever decided to do.

Halfway there, she called Cole's cell phone, not

wanting to disturb the housekeeper and Brianna if they were sleeping by ringing the house phone.

Cole answered on the second ring.

"I know it's late," she said. "But if you have a minute I'd like to talk with you."

He chuckled, and the warm sound seemed to caress her skin. "I was actually thinking about calling you, too," he said. "Polly was cleaning up in the attic today, and she found some things you might want to see."

"If you're talking about a bat population, I'm not your girl."

"I promise you it's not bats. She found some old boxes pushed back in the corner up there. I'm not sure how they were missed when we moved in, unless the movers just put some of my things in front."

"Any chance they're loaded with treasure?"

Even over the phone, she could sense his smile. "The boxes are sealed, so I guess you'll need to find out on your own."

When she arrived at the ranch, moonlight highlighted the white-fenced corrals and washed the spacious two-story house with silver. Welcoming lights blazed from the first-floor windows, and she could see Polly bustling around in the kitchen. Cole walked out to Leigh's truck to meet her, and they walked back up to the porch in companionable silence.

He flipped on a bank of switches by the door,

bathing the entire wraparound porch in soft, incandescent light, and led her to a stack of boxes he'd set beside a glass-topped patio table. "I figured I'd bring them down and save you the trip upstairs. I'll carry them out to your truck so you can look at them later, unless you're dying of curiosity right now."

"Actually, I'd rather wait. I came out because I needed to talk to you. Something my mother said made me realize that I've been wrong about a lot of things."

He shifted the boxes to the top step and offered her a seat, then took the chair next to hers, quietly waiting for her to continue.

"I left pretty fast the day Lowell was arrested. When Brianna fabricated a story about you and her mother getting back together, all I could see was a hurting young girl who would do anything to help her parents reunite. I grew up wishing I had a dad, and I know how desperate and heartbreaking those fantasies can be."

Cole's eyes grew dark and deep with understanding. "And you didn't want to be in the way?"

"Something like that…or maybe I knew I could never measure up, and it was a good excuse to run before facing yet another failure. I have no idea what it's like, being part of a normal family. My mother armed her daughters for battle in this world, not for anything approximating sentiment."

"I want to know how many people grow up in 'normal' families. What is that, exactly? I sure don't know—my mom left when I was nine, and you know about my father." Cole's smile was tinged with sadness. "I was angry at everyone and everything. Then I finally realized that I could let the past rule my life, or find a new path. If God could forgive me for everything I'd ever done and could unconditionally love me, maybe I was worth something after all. My life changed completely the day I finally made the right decision."

Leigh nodded. "That's why I came here tonight. I…I've been making the wrong ones, and I just couldn't leave things the way they were."

"You're moving your clinic back here?" he teased.

"I'm not throwing away a chance at happiness. Not this time."

"And what," he asked, "would make you happy?" He trailed a fingertip against her cheek, then tucked her hair behind her ear. "This?"

He leaned forward and brushed a gentle kiss against her lips, then gave her a second, deeper kiss, one that was filled with hope, and promise… and love. "Or this?"

She smiled, then kissed him back with all the answering love in her heart. "Definitely, that. Though maybe we should try again to be sure?"

He drew back and their eyes met. "I'm sure,

Leigh. I think I loved you from the first moment we met in high school, though I was too young and messed up to recognize it."

EPILOGUE

Fall Harvest Days was an annual event in Wolf Creek that drew people from all over the county. The local churches set up food booths and games for children. Softball and soccer teams from the county's high schools came to play for the Harvest Trophies. Keeping up with the times, the committee had added a 5K run this year.

But the event that always drew the biggest crowd was the fried-chicken dinner on Saturday night, a fund-raiser put on by the Wolf Creek Community Church. The line started forming long before the doors opened at five.

Cole looped an arm around Leigh's shoulders and gave her a hug as they stood and watched the side door of the church open and the long line of customers start down into the basement.

They'd just finished their own shift—hours of dishing up salads and desserts, setting the long tables and peeling potatoes. Brianna had been eager to help serve as well, so she would be occupied for another hour.

Michael, Janna and Rylie strolled arm in arm up Main Street, with Ian and Claire tagging along behind them, to join the end of the line.

"They look so happy, don't they?" Leigh said. "Even my mother—at least a little."

A stranger looking at Claire's dour expression might not see it, but the fact that she'd been willing to come at all would have been a surprise even a month ago.

She'd changed in subtle ways after Leigh had brought the boxes of Gray's things to her at the lodge and had helped her go through them.

There'd been nothing inside of great monetary value. One box held old sepia-toned family photos that would be a treasure to protect and enjoy for generations to come.

But it was the other box that had the greater impact.

At first, the old files inside had seemed outdated and worthless. Yellowed receipts. Copies of utility bills. Old bank statements.

A heavy file near the bottom, labeled Medical, had appeared destined for the shredder as well, until Leigh had opened it, and Gray's life—and heavy financial burdens—had unfolded before her eyes.

Breathless, she'd thumbed through page after page of monumental medical bills dating back several years before his death. He'd stamped PAID on each one, with the date—which coincided with the approximate time that he'd sold Four Winds to Cole…and which fell just three months before his death.

And beneath those were far more statements. But these dated back ten years, from his wife's cancer treatments at clinics across the United States and even some from foreign countries, where she'd apparently stayed for months at a time, in a desperate fight for her life.

The documents explained why Gray had fallen so deeply into debt, and why—when teetering on the brink of bankruptcy—he'd sold out so abruptly. The discovery had softened Claire's attitude toward Cole, even if she still harbored stony anger at her late brother.

Cole smiled down at Leigh and brushed a kiss against her cheek. "A year ago, I never would've believed that I'd be standing here with you. I love you, Leigh McAllister. Will you marry me?"

Probably from the first day they met, there'd been only one answer she could give, and that answer was…

"Yes!" And then she tipped her head up for another kiss that told him exactly how much she meant it.

* * * * *

*Danger comes to Wolf Creek, Wyoming,
once again
and Tessa McAllister meets it head on!
Look for WILDFIRE, the final book in the
SNOW CANYON RANCH trilogy,
in March 2008.*

Dear Reader,

Welcome back to Wolf Creek, Wyoming, for the second of three books involving the McAllister sisters! I love the Wyoming Rockies, and have really enjoyed writing about these strong, determined, young women who must each face challenges and danger when they move back to their hometown to help their aging mother.

In Vendetta, Leigh and Cole each have deep issues from their early lives—problems that have shaped who they are and kept them from leading the full and abundant lives of faith and joy that God wants for all of His Children. Like them, all of us face discouragement, doubt, suffering and loss at some point. But the Lord is with us through all of our own troubles, too. Trust in His love and abiding presence. Speak to Him in prayer. Then we can make it through the very worst of times!

I hope you'll come back to Wolf Creek next month, to join Tessa on her own journey through dangers she can't predict, and the return of the one man she never, ever wanted to see again.

Wishing you blessings and peace,

Roxanne

QUESTIONS FOR DISCUSSION

1. Leigh is struggling to build a new career, but someone is spreading gossip in an effort to destroy her dreams. Have you ever been the subject of unfair gossip? How can one effectively deal with the repercussions? Have you ever passed along gossip about someone else?

2. Claire McAllister continues to feel deep anger at her late brother because he sold his ranch rather than leaving it to her daughters as he'd promised. Unfortunately, it isn't uncommon for families to be at odds over an inheritance. Has that happened in your family? Were you able to resolve the situation amicably? How?

3. Cole Daniels has held on to his anger against the McAllisters for many years, blaming them for his father's unjust incarceration and subsequent death. In this story, he is on a vendetta to prove his father's innocence. What does the Bible say about forgiveness? Should Cole seek the truth about that long ago murder, or just let it go?

4. Leigh and her sisters have been estranged for many years and are now trying to break down those walls of misunderstanding. Have you

been in this type of situation? Can you ever fully repair a broken relationship?

5. Cole feels Brianna has been hurt enough by her parents' divorce and thus he tries to protect her from the fact that her mother no longer wants to be the custodial parent. Is he right in hiding the truth to save Brianna's feelings—or wrong? Have you ever been in a position where telling the truth will hurt someone badly? What did you do?

6. Leigh feels unlovable. Her own mother was cold toward her and Leigh has never had a strong romantic relationship, so she doesn't easily trust in the love offered to her. What does the Bible say about God's love for us?

7. Claire McAllister feels the world is a cruel, hard place and that her job was to help her daughters grow up to be tough, hardworking women. What do you feel about her approach to motherhood? What about your own childhood—do you wish your parents had done anything differently? Did this affect how you parented your own children?

8. Leigh feels a sense of overwhelming peace and joy at being part of the church family of her child-

hood once again. Have you developed a strong relationship with your church and its members? What can you do to strengthen those ties?

9. Leigh prays for God's assistance in a variety of situations. How are her prayers answered? How often do you pray and how has God answered?

10. The McAllister sisters have come together to watch over their stubborn, difficult mother who is showing advancing signs of dementia. It certainly isn't easy to deal with this situation, however. Do you have a chronically ill person in your family, or know of another family who does? How does this challenge affect the family as a whole? Is the burden equally shared? Discuss ways in which family members can more effectively cope with this stress, and how faith and prayer might help.

INTRODUCING

Love Inspired.
H I S T O R I C A L
A NEW TWO-BOOK SERIES.

Every month, acclaimed
inspirational authors
will bring you engaging stories
rich with romance, adventure
and faith set in a variety
of vivid historical times.

History begins on **February 12**
wherever you buy books.

Steeple
Hill®

LIHLAUNCH

www.SteepleHill.com

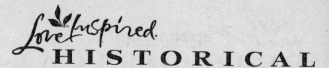

INSPIRATIONAL HISTORICAL ROMANCE

When soldier Red Meyers was wounded in World War II he felt that his sweetheart, Bertie Moenning, deserved a whole man, so he kept his distance. But a tragedy on the home front threatened both their lives and brought them back together. As they fought for survival, Red had to summon the faith and courage to protect the woman he'd never stopped loving.

Look for

Hideaway Home

by Christy Award-winning author

HANNAH ALEXANDER

Available March wherever you buy books.

Steeple Hill®

www.SteepleHill.com

LIH82783

HISTORICAL

INSPIRATIONAL HISTORICAL ROMANCE

She had made a solemn promise to see her younger sister to safety in California. But the journey across the frontier was a test of courage for Faith Beal. All she had to sustain her was the guiding hand of a stranger who truly seemed heaven-sent. But would the secrets that seemed to haunt Connell McClain threaten their growing feelings for one another?

Look for

Frontier Courtship

by

VALERIE HANSEN

Available March wherever you buy books.

Steeple
Hill®

LIH82784

REQUEST YOUR FREE BOOKS!
2 FREE RIVETING INSPIRATIONAL NOVELS
PLUS 2 FREE MYSTERY GIFTS

Love Inspired®
SUSPENSE

YES! Please send me 2 FREE Love Inspired® Suspense novels and my 2 FREE mystery gifts. After receiving them, if I don't wish to receive any more books, I can return the shipping statement marked "cancel." If I don't cancel, I will receive 4 brand-new novels every month and be billed just $3.99 per book in the U.S. or $4.74 per book in Canada, plus 25¢ shipping and handling per book and applicable taxes, if any*. That's a savings of 20% off the cover price! I understand that accepting the 2 free books and gifts places me under no obligation to buy anything. I can always return a shipment and cancel at any time. Even if I never buy another book from Steeple Hill, the two free books and gifts are mine to keep forever.

123 IDN EL5H   323 IDN ELQH

Name _____ (PLEASE PRINT)

Address _____ Apt. #

City _____ State/Prov. _____ Zip/Postal Code

Signature (if under 18, a parent or guardian must sign)

Order online at www.LoveInspiredSuspense.com
Or mail to Steeple Hill Reader Service™:

IN U.S.A.: P.O. Box 1867, Buffalo, NY 14240-1867
IN CANADA: P.O. Box 609, Fort Erie, Ontario L2A 5X3

Not valid to current Love Inspired Suspense subscribers.

Want to try two free books from another series?
Call 1-800-873-8635 or visit www.morefreebooks.com

* Terms and prices subject to change without notice. NY residents add applicable sales tax. Canadian residents will be charged applicable provincial taxes and GST. This offer is limited to one order per household. All orders subject to approval. Credit or debit balances in a customer's account(s) may be offset by any other outstanding balance owed by or to the customer. Please allow 4 to 6 weeks for delivery.

Your Privacy: Steeple Hill is committed to protecting your privacy. Our Privacy Policy is available online at www.eHarlequin.com or upon request from the Reader Service. From time to time we make our lists of customers available to reputable firms who may have a product or service of interest to you. If you would prefer we not share your name and address, please check here. ☐

LISUS07

Love Inspired

SUSPENSE

RIVETING INSPIRATIONAL ROMANCE

War hero Jude Walker returns home, hoping to reunite with
the woman he'd fallen for during his last leave. Instead, he finds
her missing, with her last known address a homeless shelter.
Sarah Montgomery, the shelter's director, knows the streets
and the dangers...but falling for him is her riskiest move yet.

Look for

MIA:
MISSING IN ATLANTA

by DEBBY GIUSTI

Available March wherever books are sold.

Steeple
Hill®

www.SteepleHill.com

LIS44284

Love Inspired SUSPENSE

TITLES AVAILABLE NEXT MONTH
Don't miss these four stories in March

WILDFIRE by Roxanne Rustand
Snow Canyon Ranch

Years ago, Josh Bryant broke Tessa McAllister's heart. When he showed up again in *her* town, Tessa counted the days until he'd leave. She had enough to handle with drought, wildfire and underhanded rivals—she couldn't bear to risk her heart again.

DON'T LOOK BACK by Margaret Daley
Reunion Revelations

Cassie Winters was overjoyed when her brother got a job as a journalist...until his latest story resulted in a fatal end. Determined to find the truth, Cassie sought help from her former professor—and not-so-former crush—Jameson King.

BROKEN LULLABY by Pamela Tracy

Growing up in the Mob had left Mary Graham with emotional scars. Still, after years in hiding, Mary had nowhere to go but home. Home offered little safety, though, and fear soon drove Mary to turn to the last man *anyone* in her family could trust—policeman Mitch Williams.

MIA: MISSING IN ATLANTA by Debby Giusti

Finally home, returning war hero Jude Walker was ready to reunite with the woman he'd met on his last leave. Her last known address, though, was a homeless shelter. Shelter director Sarah Montgomery wanted to help, but she feared it would all end in heartache...for *both* of them.